DATE DUE 2/02

GAYLORD			PRINTED IN U.S.A.

The Sundowner

G·K
Hall
&Cᵒ.

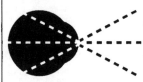
This Large Print Book carries the
Seal of Approval of N.A.V.H.

The Sundowner

Madeline Harper

G.K. Hall & Co. • **Waterville, Maine**

Published in 2002 by arrangement with Shannon Harper.

G.K. Hall Large Print Romance Series.

The text of this Large Print edition is unabridged.
Other aspects of the book may vary from the original edition.

Set in 16 pt. Plantin by Myrna S. Raven.

Printed in the United States on permanent paper.

Library of Congress Cataloging-in-Publication Data

Harper, Madeline.
    The sundowner / Madeline Harper.
      p. cm.
    ISBN 0-7838-9749-9 (lg. print : hc : alk. paper)
    1. Inheritance and succession — Fiction. 2. Seaside resorts — Fiction. 3. Florida — Fiction. 4. Large type books. I. Title.
PS3558.A6247938 S86 2002
  813'.54—dc21   2001051835

To Adele Leone with thanks

1

Kara Selwyn parked her car in the lot beside the Sundowner Bar and Grill, took off her dark glasses and gazed speculatively at the ramshackle building. It was a dump, all right, much as she had expected, but the view . . . that was more than she'd hoped for.

When she'd inherited her father's restaurant on Florida's west coast, she'd felt as if a treasure had been bestowed upon her. Property. Not only property, but property with a view of the Gulf. There'd never been a doubt in her mind what she was going to do with it.

Kara ran a comb through her hair and checked her makeup in the rearview mirror before leaving the car. The heat, even on this April morning, was intense, and she wished that she were wearing shorts and a T-shirt instead of a linen dress, hose and heels. But this was business, not pleasure, and she planned to handle herself in a professional manner. After all, she'd never closed down a business. The thought made her anxious — she hated causing anyone to lose a job — but surely the Sundowner employees realized that with her father gone, changes were inevitable. Besides, the Sundowner had been her father's baby. It meant nothing to her.

She climbed the stairs leading to a wide-planked deck that hugged three sides of the rambling cypress building. Tables were arranged haphazardly on the deck beneath faded umbrellas. There was a certain tacky charm to the run-down place — it seemed to spring naturally from the setting, much like the tangled undergrowth and immense trees that surrounded it. Sea gulls dived and swooped in the cloudless sky, and a fresh wind from the west bore the heady scent of saltwater. Kara paused for a moment to drink in the scene.

"An idyllic location — it must be worth a lot," she murmured to herself. "Almost too good to be true."

The property was more expansive than she had been led to believe, a large point of land that jutted out into the Gulf of Mexico. On one side was a canal, on the other, beyond the dirt parking lot, was a grove of cypress, live oak, scrub palmetto and palm. The view itself was spectacular. If she looked one way, she could see fishing piers surrounded by boats bobbing in the surf and, in the opposite direction, she could see a long curving shore, topped by a row of high-rise hotels. Straight ahead a long wharf protruded into the water; beyond it was only endless sea and sky.

With a satisfied smile, Kara pushed open the creaking door to the bar for her ten o'clock appointment with Nick Fleming, the manager of the Sundowner. After the brightness of the sun, she found herself squinting in the cool dim room. She had an immediate impression of dark wood, ceiling fans and the smell of stale beer mixed with the salty tang of sea air.

There was a man at the bar with his back to her, casually turning the pages of a newspaper. He didn't react when she entered, giving her a moment to quietly observe him.

He was wearing khaki cutoffs, worn-out tennis shoes, and a black T-shirt that stretched tightly over his muscular back. She had the impression of long lean muscles, darkly tanned skin and shaggy dark brown hair. She'd never cared for long hair on men, but she couldn't help noticing that the texture was nice — thick and slightly wavy.

Shaking away sensations that had no place in a business meeting, Kara cleared her throat and spoke. "Mr. Fleming," she said, attempting a crisp, authoritative voice. "I'm here for our appointment."

He swung around on the bar stool and faced her with a frown. His classically handsome face was given an edge of harshness by an imperfect nose, which looked as if it had been broken more than once. "You're a little early, aren't you?"

"No, I'm sure I arranged the appointment for ten o'clock," she said firmly. "I usually remember things like that."

"Yeah, and I usually forget." He stood up and moved toward her.

For a moment Kara was taken aback. He was tall, she realized, over six feet, fit and trim. He was also very intimidating. Maybe it was his size, or the width of his chest, or the intenseness of his dark eyes. Or maybe it was just the way he moved with a confidence that made him seem dangerous.

"Would you like a cup of coffee? The pot's brewing," he offered. His voice was low and husky. He nodded toward the huge teak bar that dominated the room. Behind it on a hot plate was a carafe of black coffee.

"No, I don't think so. I've already had my morning coffee, and it makes me, well, jittery to have more than one. . . ." Kara broke off. She was babbling in a way that sounded very unprofessional, not at all like the new and assertive owner of the Sundowner.

"I drink about three cups every morning," he said, "but it takes a lot to get me going." He smiled at her for the first time, a smile that made him look younger, softened the creases in his face and revealed deep dimples on each side of his wide, full mouth.

He looked her up and down and then to Kara's amazement began to circle around her with his swaggering gait. "So what kind of experience have you had?"

"Excuse me?" Kara asked coolly, drawing herself up to her full five feet five inches.

"Experience," he repeated, "in this kind of business." When she didn't respond he said impatiently, "You know, bars, restaurants."

"Well, none, actually, but I don't think that matters considering —"

"It matters," he interrupted, "but it's not mandatory, as long as you're good-looking, have plenty of pep and great legs, of course." He sauntered back to the bar, poured a mug of coffee and settled himself on a stool. From that vantage point, he continued to look at her expectantly.

"Good-looking? Great legs? Mr. Fleming, I think —"

Nick ignored her protestations and kept on talking. "What I see is fine. Good ankles, nice firm calves, but it's your knees and thighs I really need to check out. You'd be amazed at how many women, even at your age — around twenty-five, I'd guess — have let their thighs go." He quirked a dark eyebrow and added, "You should have worn shorts."

Kara couldn't believe what she was hearing, but she was too stunned to speak.

He continued in a conversational tone. "I guess you wanted to make a good impression. Which you have done, by the way. I like redheads, and so do the customers. Redheads are usually outgoing, friendly. They tend to have fiery dispositions, but that just adds spice to the usually lazy atmosphere around here. Now I wonder, do you have a fiery disposition, honey?"

Kara opened her mouth to respond,

searching for an expletive that was ladylike enough not to embarrass her but pithy enough to let him know she wasn't about to take any more of this nonsense. But again he didn't wait for her to find the right words.

"Now if you'll just raise your skirt up over your knees. . . ."

Kara finally exploded. "Raise my skirt over my knees? I don't believe this!" Kara was shouting, her voice echoing in the empty bar, but she didn't care. "What kind of maniac are you?" she cried. "You must be insane."

"Hey, lady, get control of yourself. It's only a waitressing job. No need to go off the deep end."

"Waitressing job?" She advanced on him with her fists clenched. She stopped a few feet away, planting herself firmly in front of him. "I'm not here about a waitressing job. I have an appointment with you, if indeed you are the manager of this establishment. My name is Kara Selwyn —"

"Good Lord." Enlightenment broke across his face. "Kara. I don't believe it. Sean's little girl." He laughed good-naturedly. "Well, hardly a little girl anymore," he amended, seemingly unperturbed by her outburst. "I know all about you, Kara. Sean was like a father to me, and he loved to talk about his little girl."

"Well, Mr. Fleming, Sean's 'little girl' owns this place now. As I mentioned in my letter setting up this appointment —"

"Letter?"

"Yes, I wrote over two weeks ago telling you that I'd be here at ten o'clock this morning to discuss business with you. I assume you read the letter," she said bluntly.

He leaned against the bar sipping his coffee. "Never assume, Kara, because I haven't read your letter. I get around to my mail once a month — about the thirtieth — pay the bills, answer what needs answering and toss the rest. So you'll understand that I haven't seen your letter yet." He checked a calendar behind the bar. "It's only April twentieth."

Kara stood dumbfounded for a moment, her hands still in tight fists.

Nick continued his explanation. "When you came in asking about an appointment, I figured you were applying for a job as bar waitress. I'd set up interviews for a little later this morning." He grinned broadly. "What I could see of you looked just right, so I'm sure you understand my mistake."

Kara couldn't even begin to respond.

"The waitress outfit is a short little skirt and halter top. Kind of a sailor costume." He grinned again. "That sort of thing draws lots of customers."

"Oh, I'll bet it does." Sarcasm dripped from each syllable. "But now you know I'm not here to apply for a job. In fact, Mr. Fleming," she added, deliberately avoiding the use of his first name, "I'm here to relieve you of a job."

"Is that so?" He raised a quizzical eyebrow.

"Yes, exactly." Kara was pleased to be back in control — voice level, pulse close to normal, hands relaxed. She felt the flush leave her face, and even managed to curve her lips into the semblance of a smile.

"As new owner of the Sundowner," she said with authority, "I am here to inform you that I'm closing it down." She was pleased to see Nick Fleming's mouth drop open in surprise. "Oh, I'll give two weeks' notice to you and the rest of the *staff*." She stressed the word to let him know she ranked his position no higher than that of a bar waitress. "That should allow you plenty of time to find other jobs. At the end of two weeks, this place will be officially closed."

"Come on now. You have to be kidding. You can't close down Sean's place. No way." He wasn't leaning casually against the bar now, but standing stiffly upright.

Kara, on the other hand, had assumed a more comfortable, confident pose. "I'm the owner," she reminded him, "and I've chosen to close down and sell the Sundowner. It's prime waterfront property, so I shouldn't have any trouble selling it to a developer. There're hungry agents out there. I'll just list it with one of them and be on my way back to Atlanta. However, I thought that I owed you and the other staff —" she smiled again "— the courtesy of a personal explanation."

Any sense of authority she'd gained was

wiped away when she saw the dark, threatening look on Nick Fleming's face. Instinctively, she took a step backward.

"Your father poured his heart and soul into this bar," he uttered angrily. "It was his life, Kara. After only ten minutes on the site, you decide to have it torn down to make way for condos."

"I . . . I'm not sure. Maybe not condos. Maybe a hotel." Kara struggled to regain her authority. "But I do know that I have no use for this ramshackle place. It outlived its usefulness long ago." She raised her chin defiantly.

"Then I pity you," Nick said, "for trying to dismiss your father so easily."

His words hit her like a blow. "That's quite enough, Mr. Fleming. You have no right —"

"I have every right," he countered. "And I'm only glad that Sean isn't here to see you now. He never would have brought you up to behave this way."

"Just a minute!" She could feel her anger rising again. "Who the hell do you think you are to talk about how my father would have brought me up? It's a moot point in any case since he didn't stay around long enough to bring me up at all." Kara felt her eyes sting. "He left that to my mother, and she did a damned good job. As for my father, I haven't seen him in almost fifteen years. . . ." She broke off quickly, afraid he would see her pain. "None of this involves you, anyway." She re-

15

gained her composure. "So just stay out of my business."

"Frankly, I'd like nothing better."

"Good," she replied icily.

"But I'm afraid I can't stay out of this." His eyes were narrow and glittered with anger. "Getting involved with a spoiled brat isn't my idea of fun, but I don't have any choice."

"Oh, yes, you do," she countered. "You can pack your bags and leave. Now. Your two weeks' notice is rescinded, Mr. Fleming. You're fired." She moved back toward him, filled with authority again. "Before I met you I felt nervous — even a little guilty — about closing the Sundowner, but you've managed to make my task easier." She gestured broadly toward the door. "So you can leave now," she demanded.

Nick shook his head. "Sorry to shatter your dramatic little scene, but I'm afraid you're not going to get your way. I'm not leaving. There's a piece of the puzzle that's still missing."

Kara frowned, wondering what he could possibly be talking about. "The letter from the bank's executor was straightforward," she said.

"Then the letter didn't cover everything."

"Perhaps not, but I saw a copy of the will. All of my father's worldly possessions were left to me. That includes the Sundowner and the land it stands on."

The smile had reappeared on Nick's face, and Kara didn't like the look of it. "Sure you don't want more coffee? Oh, I forgot," he said solicitously, "it makes you upset. Lord knows we don't want to upset you. That might bring on more histrionics. Maybe a drink?"

"It's the middle of the morning —"

"But what a morning," he interrupted. "A morning for a drink if there ever was one." He leaned back against the bar.

"I don't want a drink," she said. "What I do want is to find out about this missing piece of the puzzle, if there is such a thing. In my opinion, you're just trying to buy time."

That set him off. "All right, lady. Let's forget the games, forget the threats and forget the dramatics. This is for real. A few years ago your dad and I made a deal. He sold me half of the Sundowner."

"I don't believe it!" Kara's face turned beet red. "You're lying."

At that, Nick quickly stepped forward and grabbed her upper arms. "Just get this straight right now. Half of this bar belongs to me. I have the papers. It's all legal, and there's no way on earth I'm going to sell out to you and allow developers to move in here and tear down the Sundowner. So I suggest you get the hell out of here and go back where you came from." His dark, hard eyes held her as fiercely as his grip on her arms.

She tried to pull away, but he held fast. "You bastard," she said through clenched teeth.

With that he dropped her arms in a motion that seemed to dismiss her and everything about her. Then he turned away.

She followed, moving in front of him and facing him angrily. "You're bluffing," she cried.

"Okay, then call my bluff." He reached behind the bar for the phone, then shuffled through a pile of business cards until he found the one he wanted. "Let's go see my lawyer and find out just how much of a bluff this is."

"I wouldn't trust your lawyer on a bet," she snapped back, trying to control her shaking.

"Then get one of your own." He picked up the receiver and dialed.

Kara's anger by that time was so intense that if there had been a blunt instrument around, she would have been tempted to grab it and bring it down on Nick Fleming's head. Failing that, she moved closer to catch every word he was saying.

"Tom Melendez, please." He turned slightly so that his eyes met Kara's while he waited. "Hello, Tommy? Nick Fleming. Sean's daughter is here, and — no, Tommy, she's nothing like Sean, I can assure you that. But she's certainly interesting in her own way."

Kara refused to react to that.

"Listen, Tommy, we need to see you about those papers. Yeah, the ones I brought over for you to look at after Sean died. Seems that she's Sean's sole heir, but she doesn't understand about the bar. No, she apparently knows nothing of my partnership with her father." He listened for a moment and then looked over at

Kara. "Three o'clock, okay?"

"Three o'clock is fine," she said, barely controlling her anger. She wanted nothing more than to slap the self-satisfied smirk off Nick Fleming's face.

He hung up the phone and addressed her curtly. "Three o'clock at the Melendez law office in the Palmetto Building on First Street in Cypress Key. I'm sure you can find it."

"I'm staying at the Palms Motel on First. I can find it." Kara tried to match his curt tone. But she couldn't avoid the terrible feeling that Nick Fleming was neither lying nor bluffing. Somehow she knew she was stuck with him. Her dream had become a nightmare.

Kara took a deep breath, smoothed back her hair and said with as much aplomb as she could muster, "Then I'll see you at three o'clock. I'll call the bank first, of course, and check out your Mr. Melendez." She turned to leave.

Nick's voice followed her, low and laughing. "You do that, Kara. Oh, by the way, you still have great legs."

She stepped out into the bright sunlight and slammed the door behind her as hard as she could.

2

When Kara and Nick left the Palmetto Building together they weren't speaking.

The sun baked down, and the light breeze that rustled the leaves of the cabbage palms and palmettos did nothing to cool the air. Silently they walked to the parking lot. Arriving at her car, Kara wasn't surprised when Nick stopped at the brown Jeep parked beside her. Somehow it suited him. It bore the battle scars of a vehicle that had been worked long and hard, yet it looked clean, polished, and sturdy. Kara found herself admiring it.

When she looked over at Nick, the look of appreciation quickly faded; she didn't want him to get the idea that anything about him pleased her. Not the Jeep, and certainly not the man himself. He wore his black T-shirt again, but he'd substituted shorts for a pair of clean, well-pressed khaki trousers. His dark hair was neatly combed back, and sunglasses shielded his eyes. She looked away and reached for her car door.

"Well?" he said.

"Well, what? I'm going back to my motel."

"Without a word?" he asked.

"All right. I suppose you want me to say that you weren't lying, that my father did sell you half of the bar."

"I don't want you to say it unless you believe it."

"Obviously, I do. I checked with the bank before our meeting. And Mr. Melendez comes highly recommended. The papers he showed me are all in order. Does that satisfy you?"

"If it satisfies you, and if it means that you'll be going back to Atlanta and leave the running of the Sundowner to me."

"Wait just a minute —"

"Don't worry," he interrupted. "Everything will be on the up-and-up. Here's my deal. Each month I send you a statement of profits and a small check. The check will contain your share of the profits plus most of mine. Eventually I'll buy you out. I'd buy you out today if I had the money, but in eight or ten years — less if I can swing it — you're paid off. You're happy. I'm happy. Best of all, we never have to see each other again." He leaned his long frame against the Jeep and waited.

"That's one way to handle it. Your way. But as you might have noticed, Mr. Fleming, I don't like to do things your way. Furthermore, there's a piece of the puzzle *you* don't know about." She got a great deal of satisfaction from quoting his own line back to him. "I'm not remotely interested in a little money now and then, and knowing you — even as briefly as I do — I expect it would be very little and very infrequently. No, I'm interested in a lot of money soon. I have no intention of waiting

21

eight or ten years until you can buy me out."

Kara pushed her sunglasses on top of her head and looked up at him, narrowing her eyes in the glare. "Here's *my* deal. We contact an agent, sell the Sundowner, and split the profits. You go your way. I go mine. The ending remains the same — we never have to see each other again. I'll even give you an extra five percent just to sweeten the pot."

He shook his head. "No way. I'm not selling, and that's the final word. So it looks like we're at an impasse. What I'd really like to know is why you're so fired up to sell right away. Do you need the money or something?"

"Not that it's any of your business, but I need — I want — my share from the Sundowner for a special project that requires capital."

"What special project?" he persisted.

"As I said, it's not any of your business." She opened the car door.

"Maybe not."

"All right," she said. There couldn't be any harm in letting him know her plans. It might even make him more understanding. "The truth is, I have a background in art, and I —"

"Oh, no," he interrupted. "You're a painter. One of those artsy types. I might have known."

Kara heard the disdain in his voice and berated herself for thinking he would understand anything about her. "No, Mr. Fleming, I'm not a painter, but I majored in art history in college. I've been working as assistant manager in a gallery for the past two years. It's not satisfying for me creatively." She didn't add that the salary was minuscule and that she and the owner differed frequently — and vehemently — on every aspect of the business.

"Then let me guess," Nick said. "You want to open a place of your own, right? You want to be in charge, do it your way."

"You're smarter than you look, Mr. Fleming, which of course isn't saying much," she answered. "I do want to open my own gallery. I have the contacts, the knowledge and the style."

"I see. I suppose you have plans to promote some young, handsome starving artist who, in return, would show you his gratitude."

She didn't bother to show offense at that tasteless remark. "If I were to promote any artists, it would be because they were talented. But none of this concerns you. All I need from you is an agreement to sell the Sundowner."

He shook his head. "Why don't you borrow the money from stepdaddy?"

"My stepfather isn't in the habit of lending money," she said tersely. "Besides, I have no need to borrow. I own half of the Sundowner."

"You'd really sell it and throw your share away on a venture like that?" he asked in disgust. "There must be dozens of galleries in Atlanta."

"Hundreds, actually."

"All struggling along for a share of the few

people who like art."

"Obviously you have no understanding of the subject, and I'm not taking the time to educate you. After all," she added mockingly, "I don't have the lifetime it would require. The point is, half the Sundowner is mine, and when we sell it, I can use the money for anything I want. I don't need your permission, do I?"

Standing in the parking lot with the sun beating down was beginning to get to Kara, and Nick didn't seem ready to give up the battle.

"You still don't understand, do you, Kara?" There was a deep undertone of anger in his voice. "The Sundowner isn't just a building. It's a home. To me and many other people."

"You weren't born there. You probably just stumbled onto it. You can just as easily stumble off to some other place. With all your talent," she added sarcastically, "you can find another bar to manage."

He didn't answer, but his hard expression deepened.

It didn't stop Kara. "I'm right, aren't I? You just appeared out of the blue and wormed your way into my father's affections."

He flinched slightly, but then responded openly. "Actually, I did stumble onto the place. I was out of work, Sean hired me and liked me, and gradually I took on more and more responsibility. He needed a partner to help him out, and I was there. In case you think there's something dishonest involved, you're mistaken. For seven years I put most of my salary back into the Sundowner. I worked hard for my share of the place, Kara."

"And I didn't. Is that it?" she shot back, wondering why everything he said made her defensive.

"The Sundowner was a way of life for Sean. It was all he had. I never let him down."

"The way I did?"

"You said it, not me. But the fact that you didn't even show up for his funeral —"

She bristled at that. "Did you ever think of asking why? Well, I'll tell you. I wasn't even in the country at the time. I didn't know he'd died until a week after. Otherwise I'd have been here."

"Would you?" Nick asked.

"This is ridiculous. You have no right to grill me," Kara snapped.

"Don't I?"

"I don't have to stand here in this heat and listen to your insinuating questions, which I haven't the slightest intention of answering. I'm going back to my motel to have a cool bath and to think things over. I'd suggest you do the same."

A risqué smile twitched the corners of his mouth. "Really? You want me to go back to your motel for a cool bath? Now that's the best idea I've heard all day." He looked up at the cloudless sky. "With all that hot sun pounding down, splashing around in a bathtub with you would be just the thing."

She decided not to hit him. Not in public. Certainly not in the parking lot of his lawyer's office. Instead, she pulled her sunglasses back down and got into the car. With as much coolness as she could muster, she said, "As you very well know, I'm going to my room *alone*." She didn't wait for his response but went right to what mattered. "When I get there, I'm going to think of a solution to this mess. And *that* is what I'm talking about when I suggest you do the same."

His smile widened.

She continued. "I'll see you tomorrow. Let's try to discuss things calmly and thoughtfully and share our ideas in a civilized way." That was more like it. She was beginning to sound professional and businesslike again.

"Okay." Seemingly unimpressed, Nick shrugged. "Suit yourself, Kara, but there's just one solution — for you to go back to Atlanta and leave me and the bar in peace."

Kara started the engine and threw the car into gear. Nick had to move away quickly as she sped out of her parking place.

"Missed him," she muttered. "Dammit."

When she arrived at her room in the Palms Motel, Kara went straight to the air conditioner and turned it on high. Then she left to fetch a bucket of ice and a soft drink. Back in her room, she poured the drink into an ice-filled cup and took a long swig.

It was time for that relaxing bath. She turned on the water in the tub and stripped off her pale blue linen dress, leaving it in a heap on the floor. After removing her underclothes and stockings, she put the drink on the side of the tub and slid into the cool water.

After a few moments of total relaxation Kara turned her mind to the subject at hand. She had to think of some way to make it all work out, some way to persuade Nick to sell the Sundowner.

She'd told Nick the truth about what she planned to do with her share. What she hadn't told him was that she'd already walked out of her job.

She'd wanted to quit for months. After learning about the inheritance, she'd finally had the courage to let her boss know what she thought of him: he bought second-rate work and sold it at exorbitant prices, he catered to customers shopping for paintings to match their decor, he never tried to educate his clients, and he ignored the really exciting artwork that was being produced in Atlanta. Galerie Moderne was a joke. Galerie Ancienne was more appropriate, she'd always told her friends.

What would she tell them now? Her ideas about the gallery, her plans to strike out on her own — none of it mattered. She was out of a job with no chance of getting a recommendation, and all her plans were being shot down by a muscular ne'er-do-well who called a run-down bar home.

Kara sank deeper into the cool water with a sigh. She had to have the Sundowner money to get started on her own. It was her only chance. That much Kara knew because she'd already exhausted all other possibilities.

She'd gone to her stepfather first, but James Selwyn III had firm ideas about lending money. He didn't do it, not even for his stepdaughter, and certainly not to support a scheme as iffy as opening another art gallery in a city already overrun with them.

He'd always been generous with Kara, paying for everything as she was growing up, from ballet lessons to orthodontia, treating her as a daughter. He'd sent her to the best private school, paid for her college education and a year of study abroad at the University of Florence. He'd even sprung for vacations; she'd been on a skiing trip to Switzerland, all expenses paid by James Selwyn, when her father died.

It wasn't difficult to figure her stepfather out: he was simply a man who liked to be in control, and a man in control doesn't make loans — to anyone. So he'd turned her down, and so had the bank. Then she'd inherited the Sundowner, and it had seemed as if her prayers were answered.

Kara drank the rest of her soda and slowly climbed out of the tub, wrapping herself in the skimpy motel towel. The way she figured it there were now two choices left for her. The first one was not acceptable. She simply couldn't agree to go back to Atlanta where she would sit around and wait for a monthly percentage of the Sundowner's profits — for the next ten years or more. She shuddered at the thought. Besides, the measly profits would probably get eaten up by fees to lawyers and accountants trying to keep tabs on Nick.

That left the other choice. Kara toweled off her hair and walked naked to the closet. She'd brought only enough clothes for a few days, the time she imagined it would take to list the Sundowner with an agent and take care of any unexpected problems. Well, there was only one problem, and he was a big one. The only course of action would be to stay in Cypress Key . . . and that's what she was going to do.

There was no way of knowing what might happen. Maybe she could wear Nick down by just being around. Maybe he'd go sailing on the Gulf of Mexico and never come back. Maybe. . . . No use trying to analyze it. She was staying and that was that.

The next morning Kara walked into the Sundowner at precisely ten o'clock. Nick was nowhere to be seen. No surprise. Obviously he didn't relish the same scene as yesterday.

She walked through the bar to the outside deck and saw him right away, strolling on the stretch of white beach that formed a crescent in front of the Sundowner. It was a beautiful day, and Nick was ambling along, kicking at the sand like a kid, apparently without a care in the world. A strange-looking yellowish dog followed at his heels.

"Nick —" she called out to him, and he crossed the beach and climbed the stairs to the deck. This morning he was dressed in a white T-shirt and cutoffs. He was barefoot.

"So you've decided not to be so formal. I'm 'Nick' today. We're making progress."

He opened the door, and they walked into the Sundowner, settling on stools at the bar. The yellow dog followed and sat at Nick's feet.

Kara took a moment to survey the bar. It was spotlessly clean, the glasses gleaming in shiny rows, the liquor bottles neatly arranged, and the stainless steel sink scrupulously clean. Kara ran her finger along the teak bar. It shone with polishing.

Nick, whom she realized had watched her inspection, asked, "Surprised? I take pride in my belongings, Kara."

"That's good to know," she said dismissively, "but we really need to talk, Nick."

He reached over the bar and poured himself a cup of coffee, not bothering to offer her one this time. "If you mean we need to argue, I think we've had enough of that."

"So do I," she replied.

"Then we're agreed. I'm sure that during

your cool bath at the motel yesterday, you came to the right conclusion — that you should take my offer. Tommy can draw up the papers."

"I'm sure he can, but he would be wasting his time because I'm staying."

Nick's cup was halfway to his mouth. "You're *what?*"

"I'm staying. This place was my father's and I've decided to hold onto my half. Don't be so shocked, Nick. After all, you've been upbraiding me for wanting to sell," she reminded him. "So it looks as though you and I will be working together."

The dog got up, licked Nick's hand and began nuzzling him. "Sit, Topaz." The dog obeyed, sort of. This time he settled down by Kara's feet. "What are you talking about?" Nick asked.

"I've decided to stay here and manage my share of the Sundowner," Kara replied. "That way, I'll have a good idea of the business we do." She threw that *we* in casually, but he blanched at the sound of it. "I'd like to see the books, of course," she added. When he didn't respond, she looked at him and asked mockingly, "Is the coffee making you a little tense, Nick?"

"You're out of your mind," he growled. "You can't mean this."

"Believe me, Nick. I mean every word. I own half the place, and I have every right to be here. Don't bother reaching for the phone," she advised. "I've already called Tom Melendez, and he thinks this is a perfect solution."

"No!" Nick slammed his coffee mug down on the bar, splattering coffee along its shiny surface and causing Topaz to snuggle even closer to Kara. She reached down and petted him. After all, the poor dog shouldn't have to suffer for his master's bad manners.

"Hell, no," he fumed. "I won't allow it. Tell me you're not serious. Tell me this is some kind of sick joke." But even as he spoke, Nick knew she wasn't joking. She'd had time to think, and this was the plan she'd come up with — taking over half the Sundowner, horning in on his life, driving him crazy.

He narrowed his eyes slightly as they met hers. Maybe that was it, maybe she thought that by driving him crazy she could drive him out. Thoughtfully, he picked up a damp cloth and wiped up the coffee. Then he poured another cup and took a deep breath. She was getting to him, just as she had yesterday, and he didn't like that. He needed to stay calm; he needed to be in control.

"I'm very surprised that you would want to stay around here, Kara," he said, smiling pleasantly. "I didn't think you liked me very much."

"Oh, I don't," she answered, "but I'm doing what has to be done. In time you'll also realize it's for the best."

He couldn't respond to that. Instead, he asked, "Don't you have a job or a house or

32

something in Atlanta to go home to?"

"Nope, not a thing," she said brightly. "I quit my job when I found out about the inheritance, and I've decided to sublet my apartment for as long as I stay here, for as long as it takes."

"Kara, for God's sake —" He couldn't believe this woman was actually going to invade his life. It was too absurd.

"You think I'm joking, don't you? You think that because I have a rich stepfather I don't need this place." She gestured broadly around the room, causing Topaz to get up again. "But despite what you may have heard from Sean about my stepfather, he hasn't handed me the world on a silver platter."

Nick had heard plenty about her stepfather. He'd heard about how Sean's wife had left him when he put their life savings into the Sundowner. She'd taken the baby girl with her, divorced Sean and remarried within a year to a man who was all the things Sean wasn't — sophisticated and successful.

There'd been bitterness, Nick knew, and Sean had always blamed James Selwyn for not letting him have access to his daughter. Of course, Kara probably had a very different story. But none of that mattered now because — by some bizarre twist of fate — Sean's daughter was planning to stay and to run the Sundowner.

"It doesn't make sense, Kara," he said finally. "Last night you wanted nothing more than to sell the place. Now I'm to believe you want to help run it. It doesn't figure."

"You've left me no choice, Nick. I can't buy you out, you won't sell out, and I refuse to walk away. Oh, I probably could get a lawyer, go to court and file petitions and suits. That way, I probably could drive you out. But frankly, I can't afford it."

Nick was silent. He couldn't think of any way to talk her out of it. All he knew was he didn't want her to start messing around with the Sundowner. "Listen, Kara," he said finally. "Sean and I had a good thing going here. We worked a certain way —"

"Oh, don't worry," she said. "I just want to observe for a while. I don't plan any changes. At least not right away," she added with a wave of her hand.

Nick wasn't fooled for a minute. Unless he fought her tooth and nail, she'd probably turn the whole place upside down.

"Okay," he said wearily. "So you're staying. But *where* are you staying? Do you have a place to live?"

She shook her head.

"There're some nice apartments along the beach . . ."

"Too expensive," she answered emphatically. "Remember, until I sublet, I'm still paying rent in Atlanta. But there's an apartment here where my father lived, isn't there?"

"Yes, upstairs."

34

"Then I'll live there."

"Uh-uh," he said. "I'm living there, and I don't plan to move out." As much as he hated to admit it, he didn't have much control over the fact that Kara was a partner. But there was one thing for sure — she'd never kick him out of his apartment, his home.

"Oh," she hesitated a moment and then said, "I thought maybe since I'm Sean's daughter and all, that —"

"No." It was his turn to be emphatic. "Not a chance. Possession is nine-tenths of the law, and I'm staying there." Then he raised one eyebrow suggestively. "Of course, you can move in with me. My bed is big and wide and has a view of the Gulf."

"In your dreams," she said flatly.

She'd met his eyes straight-on, and he got a terrible shock. He'd looked at her before, up and down, carefully, and found her to be quite a number in spite of her attitude. But he hadn't let himself look right into her eyes before. Now he did. They were Sean's eyes, blue and clear and slightly mischievous. He never was sure what really lay behind Sean's blue-eyed stare, and he certainly couldn't read Kara's.

"I can always sleep in my car," Kara said with a shrug.

Nick sighed. "I suppose you can move into my old place out on the river. It's small but adequate. And I'll let you stay for free."

She smiled at him, her first real smile — not

that forced, pained little smirk she'd given him yesterday — but a smile that lit up her face. He realized how lovely she really was.

"Thanks, Nick. I appreciate that." He forced himself not to get taken in by her smile. "What's next on the agenda?"

"Well, you've already met one of the *staff*, as you call us. I guess I'll take you to meet the rest."

She slid off the stool, and Nick let himself see the rest of her, the woman he'd glanced at briefly the day before but managed to ignore today.

What he noticed now was terrific. She was wearing shorts, but not the skimpy ones the girls wore around the Sundowner. These were white linen and came midway down her thighs. He wouldn't mind seeing the rest of those thighs, but somehow just this peek was more interesting than he would have expected — not quite enough to satisfy, but more than enough to tempt. The fact was, she looked sexy plus something else that seemed to radiate from within — young, vibrant, vivacious. Then she turned slightly, and he noticed the way the shorts clung to her rear, and that did it. She was a complete package, no doubt about it.

Kara saw his glance and teased, "Do I pass inspection? Good enough to wait tables at the Sundowner?"

Nick caught himself before he let out a wolf whistle. Instead, he decided to try for gallantry.

If he had to work with Kara — at least until he could figure out a way to get rid of her — he might as well try to make it pleasant.

"You pass inspection with flying colors," he said. "In fact, you look good enough to run the place. Come on," he invited. "The kitchen crew should be in by now. Let's go meet them." He beckoned for her to follow.

3

Kara followed Nick through the swinging doors, across the dining room and toward the kitchen. What she saw on the way wasn't encouraging. She wrinkled her nose in distaste at the checked oilcloths on the tables, the mismatched chairs, the tacky plastic flowers so ridiculous in a world filled with natural foliage.

Although the dining room was clean, the decor was so out-of-date it looked as though it had come straight out of the Great Depression. But there was one redeeming quality that couldn't be tampered with. The view of the Gulf through the floor-to-ceiling windows. It was there to stay, and it was spectacular.

Yes, she decided, the Sundowner had possibilities.

Nick waited by the kitchen door as she made her way slowly across the large room. Kara didn't care if he watched her size up the place. That's what she was here for, and he better start getting used to it.

"So, what's the verdict?" he asked as she approached.

"I'll withhold my comments until I've seen everything and talked with everyone," she told him.

"And then?" He was standing by the door,

but he hadn't made a move to open it.

"It depends," she answered cryptically.

"I'll bet," he replied, pushing the door open. "Now why don't you come on in and meet Arthur. I expect he'll get some reaction from you."

Curious, Kara followed Nick into the kitchen.

Lined with stainless steel appliances the room impressed her as being modern and efficient. That surprised her a little.

The chef was standing at one of the counters, an extremely tall, thin, middle-aged man with smooth, dark skin. There were two aspects of his appearance that brought him out of the ordinary. He was dressed entirely in white: white cotton pants, a white T-shirt, a spotless white apron. And he was totally bald.

"Meet our chef, Arthur Lapierre," Nick said, "Arthur, this is Kara, Sean's daughter."

Arthur didn't put down the sharp-bladed knife he wielded, but he looked at Kara from his great height and said, in the lilting rhythm of the Caribbean, "Well, well, Sean's little girl."

Kara nodded, not quite ready to respond. She was a little intimidated by the man.

"Mighty sorry about your dad," Arthur said. "He was the best."

"Thank you. I appreciate that," Kara answered. "I'm happy to meet you . . . Arthur," she managed. It would have felt more comfortable calling him Mr. Lapierre, but Kara was determined to show a modicum of authority even though she didn't feel it in the man's presence.

Nick, irritatingly casual, went over to the commercial-sized refrigerator, opened it and peered inside. "Shrimp look good, Art."

"Yep, they sure do," was the laconic reply, as Arthur picked up a white fish, gutted it, and with two more quick movements deboned the fish and tossed it in a pile beside the sink.

Kara watched, mesmerized.

"Well, I just thought you two should meet," Nick said. He gave Kara a little nudge toward the door.

"Much obliged," Arthur said, dismissing them and going on with his work.

Nick started toward the door, but Kara didn't follow. "Wait a minute," she said. "Shouldn't you tell Arthur what's going on?"

"Later," Nick responded, trying to get her out the door, with no success.

"I think this is a good time," Kara said. She saw no reason to put off sharing her news with the chef. She didn't expect he'd be any less intimidating an hour — or a week — from now.

"I wouldn't insist if I were you, Kara."

Arthur picked up another fish, scaled it quickly and then stopped, waiting for the two of them to come to an agreement.

Kara was a little confused about the scene. Here she was arguing with Nick while their chef looked on. This wasn't what she'd planned.

"As your partner, I must insist," Kara said.

"All right," Nick replied. "You asked for it." He addressed Arthur. "Kara brought me some very interesting news this morning."

Arthur put down his knife.

"She's going to stay in Cypress Key and work here with us at the restaurant."

"What do you mean by that, Nick?" Arthur asked.

"She's half owner of the Sundowner, and so she'll be taking over some responsibilities."

"Not in my kitchen, she won't," Arthur announced, his deep brown eyes flashing.

Startled, Kara remained silent.

"I run the kitchen, Nick," he continued. "Always have, and always will. That's the way Sean wanted it. I'm in charge back here — you're in charge out front."

"I know that," Nick said. "But now that Kara's arrived, we'll both have to give a little."

"*You* can give a little, or a lot. Not me, not in my kitchen." He went back to work then with a kind of finality that amazed Kara. He obviously had no intention of listening to anything she had to say.

"I'm not ready to make changes, Arthur," Kara attempted. "But if I could just see a menu —"

Nick heaved an audible sigh.

"Menus are out on the tables. Look all you want, but don't mess with my kitchen. I got all the help I need around here. Got two kids to bus tables and help me keep the place clean. Got waitresses to serve the food. *My* food," he added stubbornly.

"Well, I wouldn't think of interfering with any of your help," Kara tried again, "but that doesn't mean I can't offer suggestions. Adding something new —"

Arthur put down his knife and crossed his long arms. For a moment he stood like that, looking down at Kara, frowning stubbornly. Then he spoke. "I've been a chef in Miami, and I've been a chef in New Orleans. I've studied all kinds of cooking."

"I'm sure —"

Nick leaned against the door and watched. He obviously didn't want to get involved any further.

Arthur barely paused. "I know about *nouvelle cuisine,* creole and Asian, and I want to tell you here and now that there'll be no brie cheese cooked in puff pastry in my kitchen."

"No, I'm sure —"

"I'm not interested in smoked salmon on a bed of Bibb lettuce topped with a dollop of seasoned mayonnaise, either."

"I understand —"

"Crab cakes with jalapeño and lime dressing are not my style."

"They're not mine, either," Kara admitted, wondering if he'd go on indefinitely.

"Here we fry fish and we fry chicken. We don't serve kiwi." He paused, but before Kara

42

could comment, added, "And I know Greek cooking too. So don't think of suggesting I wrap leaves around anything in *my* kitchen."

This time when Nick reached for her arm, Kara didn't object. "Uh, Kara, why don't you come out to the dining room for a minute?" he suggested. "I need to talk to you."

She readily agreed, but as they turned to leave Arthur called out after them, "And there'll be no smoked trout garnished with chive blossoms around here."

Back in the dining room with the door closed behind them, Nick said, "I guess you understand the problem now."

"Oh, I understand perfectly," Kara said. Under different circumstances she would have been amused. But Kara knew what was happening.

"Before I even have a chance to look at his menu, the chef is telling me what I can't do."

"He's been in charge back there for a long time," Nick reminded her.

"And, as he said, you've been in charge out here."

"That's right," Nick agreed. "But there's really nothing to change in the bar or the restaurant. You said yourself —"

"I said that I was reserving comment," Kara reminded him. She knew that, in a different way, Nick was going to be as adamant as Arthur. Well, they weren't going to shut her out.

"Let's hear it then," he suggested.

"Not now," Kara said. "I still need to look around." This wasn't the time to argue with Nick. That would get her nowhere; and she'd already made the mistake of moving too fast once today. She'd have to practice subtlety and wait for her chance.

If he'd ever let her have it.

"Folks around here like the atmosphere just fine," he hinted.

"Atmosphere?" she blurted out. Kara couldn't help it. The word didn't fit with anything she saw, especially when a scraggly dog was sitting in the middle of the dining room. "Maybe I'll look around a bit more, try to capture some of the 'atmosphere'," she added wryly.

"Suit yourself," Nick said. He'd heard the sarcasm in her voice and the steely glint in his eyes told her he didn't like it.

"I'll also take Arthur up on his suggestion to look over the menu. It sounds fascinating. So many fried things, one hardly sees that anymore," Kara said haughtily.

His voice was as cool as her own. "Sounds like a good idea. I'll just go check out the supplies with Art."

That was no surprise. They obviously had a lot to talk about. "See you later," Kara said.

Nick strode into the kitchen with an apology on his lips. "Sorry, pal. I had no idea she was going to decide to stay. Problem is, she has a legal right. That's the damnedest thing."

"I don't care what she does, long as she's not messing in my kitchen."

"I'm not too fond of the idea of her hanging around out front, either."

"That's your problem. Just don't let her in here." Arthur hacked a little harder than necessary with his fillet knife.

"Keep cool, Arthur." The chef was famous for his temperamental outbursts, and his threats to walk out if anyone interfered in his domain were legendary. Of course, he'd never carried through with the threats because he'd always been loyal to Sean. It was no surprise to Nick that the loyalty didn't extend to Sean's interfering daughter.

"I'll keep her away," Nick promised, "if I can."

"You'd better."

"Look, she's trouble, Arthur." So was Arthur, for that matter. But if he had to choose, he'd take the chef's kind of trouble any day. "But don't worry," he soothed. "She's not going to cause any problems for you." Nick gave his chef a friendly slap on the shoulder, then added with an uncharacteristic show of emotion, "The Sundowner couldn't get along without you."

"I don't want to leave," Arthur admitted. "This old place is home for me, too. I like my life here just fine. It's comfortable for me. I hope we can keep it that way."

"Don't worry, my man. We'll think of a solution."

"Such as?" Arthur had given up all pretext of working. Now, with arms folded, he was watching Nick.

"For now I think we'll have to go with the flow. Let her think she has a role here. Keep her bogged down in trivial work, and maybe she'll get tired."

"I hear you, boss," Arthur said, chuckling musically.

"She seems fascinated with food, so maybe you can come up with something harmless to keep her occupied."

"I'll think about it," Arthur said, "but I have a feeling she won't discourage easily. Seems like a stubborn woman to me."

"But look who she's up against."

Arthur chuckled again. "You got a point there."

"So it's your job to distract her. I'll do the rest. And believe me, Art, I can outlast her. She's nothing but a spoiled brat who's making us suffer because she can't have things her way. In two weeks, she'll turn tail and head home to mama and stepdaddy and her artsy crowd in Atlanta. Everything will be back to normal then."

"Hope you're right, boss."

"Trust me. She's not going to like the restaurant business or Cypress Key. I'll see to that."

Nick found Kara on the porch. The dog, who had not followed him to the kitchen, was at her feet.

"Topaz likes you," Nick said.

"So it seems."

"He doesn't take to just anyone," he added.

"I'm flattered," Kara responded. Judging from the steely look Nick gave her, he certainly didn't miss her sarcasm. Well, that was just fine; she wouldn't have to bother with spelling out her feelings.

Then he caught her completely off guard.

"It's a beautiful morning, why don't I take you out to your new digs?"

"It's almost lunchtime. Don't you have to work?" she asked.

"Nope. Buck, our bartender, is coming in early. He can double as host and handle things without me. I'd enjoy taking some time off to show you around."

Kara stood up. "Then I'm ready. I'd love to see my new home. My *temporary* home," she added when she saw the look on his face. "In fact, I might as well start getting settled in right away."

"Might as well," he agreed.

They strode along the deck side by side, the overhanging foliage creating a green canopy above them.

"Pretty nice, isn't it?" he asked. "Closest we'll ever get to paradise."

"Yes, it's lovely. I can see why tourists choose this part of the world for vacations. But I'd expect a native like you to be used to it."

"I guess a native would be used to it," he

said. "But I come from a place that looks nothing like this — the coalfields of Pennsylvania."

That surprised her. But he didn't allow time for comment. "Why don't you follow me in your car. But stick close so you don't get lost."

"No problem," Kara said as she headed toward the car. "I can't wait to see the place."

They traveled in tandem along the coast for a while before turning off on a dirt road that was more bumps, ruts and potholes than it was road. Kara was beginning to have grave misgivings about her new home when she saw a trailer ahead under a grove of palms. Then the misgivings became serious. There was no way she was going to live in a trailer out in the middle of nowhere.

She was just starting to formulate some choice words to deliver to Nick when she realized that the trailer was not their destination. Nick's Jeep slowed down only long enough for him to yell greetings to the elderly couple working in their garden. Then he drove on for another half mile or so. Finally he stopped beneath some huge live oaks and climbed out.

Mystified, Kara got out of her car and joined him. There was no house anywhere in sight, only a slow-moving, sluggish river, deep and dark, that looked like the perfect breeding place for alligators, not to mention mosquitoes and snakes. She gave a little shudder and wondered what the hell Nick was up to.

"Over there," Nick said with a nod in the direction of the river.

She peered through the thick foliage of wild banana trees but saw nothing. "Where?" she asked, looking up and down the riverbank.

"On the river."

"*On* the river?" Moving forward she looked again and saw something white out on the water. It bobbed up and down. A boat — small, dumpy and badly in need of paint.

"That's it?" she asked. "That's my *house?* Surely you don't expect me to live on a boat?"

Nick fought back a smile. "Welcome home, Kara."

"You can't be serious," she said. "I'm not about to live there."

"Why not? It's a *house*boat, after all."

"But look at it," she cried.

He looked. "Look at what?"

"It's so . . . so . . ."

"Homey," he finished for her. "Hey, this is my old pad you're talking about. I've spent some happy times here. Of course, if you're too good for it. . . ." He let the words hang in the air. "Then maybe you ought to think about going back to Atlanta."

"Not on your life," Kara said between clenched teeth. She knew what he was up to. He wanted to shock her, discourage her, drive her away. He wanted her to give up. Well, she knew his game now, and she was ready to play — but by *her* rules.

"A houseboat," she said slowly. "How ingenious. How unusual. How . . . well, words fail me." She managed a half smile. "Let's go see it."

"Follow me." He led her around the banana patch along a path of crushed shells toward the boat.

"I just have one question, Nick," she said, as they approached the dock where the boat was moored. "Is it safe out here?" She gestured to the dark, lonely surroundings and then looked up at him, her eyes large and innocent. "For a woman alone?" Maybe the helpless female ploy would work.

He didn't seem the slightest bit concerned. "Of course it's safe."

"Of course?"

"Sure. Hardly anyone ever comes down here."

"But suppose someone does?" She was serious now.

"Don't worry, you have Kyle."

In response to her quizzical look, he said, "Kyle and Eileen, up the road in the trailer. They keep track of everyone, and if they see a strange car drive by, Kyle investigates — with his shotgun."

"Oh, great," Kara said.

"It is great. He's your protection. They also have a telephone you can use. All in all, this is probably a lot safer than living in Atlanta. But if you're really nervous —" he shrugged "—

maybe Cypress Key isn't the place for you."

"I'm not the slightest bit nervous," Kara lied. "You've allayed all my fears." She followed him onto the houseboat.

There was a small covered deck on the bow with a ladder leading to a sundeck topside. Even though it was in need of painting, the houseboat did have a kind of wayward charm.

Nick reached for the key, hidden on a high ledge. As he opened the screen door, he made a quick swipe with his hand.

"What — ?"

"Just a lizard," he explained. "They're plentiful around here. In fact, you might find a few of them have taken up housekeeping in your galley." He ushered her inside. "But don't worry. They won't bite."

"Thanks. That's encouraging."

Nick began opening windows to let in the breeze, before she had a chance to comment on the damp musty smell in the cabin.

There was only one room, about eight by twelve feet, outfitted with a built-in bunk bed that doubled as a sofa, a table that folded into the wall, and several chairs. There was also a bookcase beside the bed and drawers under the bunk. In the rear was a narrow galley with a stove, miniature refrigerator and sink, all in a row. On the opposite wall near the tiny bathroom was something that looked remotely like an air conditioner.

"Cozy," Kara said as she walked through the

galley and out onto the rear deck. It was uncovered and gave a view of the river stretching into the distance. She felt a little shiver go through her at the primitive beauty that surrounded them. The feeling was unlike anything she'd ever experienced before, and yet somehow it made her uneasy. Maybe that was because Nick, who had followed her out, was standing close beside her.

Then a fish jumped in the water, and Kara gave a start. He put a comforting hand on her shoulder, but Kara didn't feel particularly comforted. She moved away.

"It was just a fish," Nick said, "not an alligator. Although there are some around. Goes with the territory." When Kara didn't react, he added, "We haven't seen a man-eater around here in a couple of years." He grinned at her as he opened a trap door in the deck. "I'm hooking you up to the power pole over by the road so you'll have electricity. You also have auxiliary batteries if you decide to take the boat for a river cruise."

"That's not on my agenda," Kara replied, then asked, "What about water?"

"You can hire Kyle at a nominal fee to keep the tanks on the roof filled. For further comfort, I've installed a small air-conditioning unit in the kitchen."

"I saw it. It looks pretty old."

"Oh, it'll work great. No problem. I promise," Nick answered as they returned to the cabin. "There're sheets and towels under the bed, dishes and flatware in the cabinet." He sank down on the bed, testing its comfort. "Now what else do you need? I'm here for you," he said.

Kara read the flirtation in his eyes and responded quickly, "Whatever it might be, I can get at the store."

"I'm sure you'll be comfortable. It's very cozy here — and very romantic," he added, "with the water lapping against the sides of the boat, the wind whispering in the trees. Brings back wonderful memories."

"I'm sure," Kara said disinterestedly as she tried to walk past him.

His long stretched-out legs blocked her way. He was so close he could easily have reached out and touched her, pulled her down on the bed beside him.

He made no move to do so but looked up at her instead, running his eyes along her body. His lips curved in a half smile.

Damn him, she thought, he knew she was uncomfortable and yet he persisted. Nervously, she wet her lips with her tongue and started to speak.

He beat her to it. "Want me to help you make the bed?"

"I can do that myself, thank you," she said in as businesslike a tone as she could muster. Then, deciding that the cabin was too small for both her and Nick Fleming, she suggested,

"Why don't you go on back to work and let me get organized here?"

"Are you throwing me out, Kara?" He inched his foot closer and ran it along hers.

Kara kicked it away. "Yes, Nick, I'm throwing you out. This ploy of yours —"

"What ploy?" he asked innocently, leaning back, hands behind his head.

She tried not to notice the muscles in his chest beneath the tight T-shirt.

"What ploy?" he persisted.

"Any of them. All of them. First you bring me to this — this place and expect me to cringe in horror and run home. Well, that's not going to happen since I see living on this houseboat as a temporary arrangement. Then you come on to me with your sexual innuendos. I guess you think if you try to seduce me, I'll — I'll —"

"Succumb?" he finished for her. "Not you, Kara. You're much too uptown and sophisticated to fall for my ploys."

She hated the mocking, teasing tone in his voice. All she wanted was to get away from him. But when she moved back, he stood up and followed.

"You're right, I'm not falling for it," she said, looking directly at him. That was a mistake. It forced her to really notice his eyes for the first time. They weren't as dark as she'd thought but lightened by flecks of green and gold. He had a scar along his cheek and another smaller one near his mouth. His mouth was beautiful. The thought came unbidden and she pushed it away.

Nick lifted his hand and ran his fingers along the edge of her cheek. "I don't know why you would think I'm trying to seduce you, Kara," he said.

She could feel herself blushing and cursed the emotions that caused it.

"But if you're really interested, we could work something out," he continued in a husky voice.

She slapped his hand away. "In your dreams, Nick Fleming. Now, I'd really like to get settled in, so why don't you go on back to work? I'm sure your talents are needed at the Sundowner. There's a new waitress to get fitted into her little costume, isn't there?"

Nick stepped back, his eyes laughing. "You're right. There's work to do that I've been neglecting ever since you arrived on the scene. See you tonight at dinner?"

"I'll be there," she said, following him out onto the deck. "Ready to work."

Halfway to his Jeep, Nick turned back and called out to her. "And Kara, about this seduction thing. Why don't you go ahead and give it a try? I'm not easy, honey, but I'm worth the effort."

She looked around but couldn't find anything to throw at him.

4

Kara never made it back to the Sundowner. By the time she moved from the motel, shopped and met her neighbors, it was well past six o'clock. Besides, the idea of having another sparring match with Nick was about as appealing as getting in the ring with a heavyweight boxing champion.

Instead, she drove back to her neighbors' place, planning to leave a message at the Sundowner for Nick that she wouldn't return until the next day. She was sure he would be delighted.

"Honey, you can use our phone anytime," Kyle assured her. "We're just happy to see someone enjoying the boat again."

"We sure are," his robust wife agreed. "Nice to have company, too."

With the couple's permission she made two more calls, one to the lawyer, Tom Melendez, and the next to an accountant Tommy recommended. She made an appointment with the accountant for the next morning. After chatting for a while with her neighbors, she was ready to leave. But Kyle and Eileen didn't make it easy.

Eileen had just fried a batch of chicken. "Sure you don't care for a piece?" she asked.

"No, really. I just bought a load of groceries

and some fresh shrimp."

"How you plan to cook 'em?"

"I thought I'd just boil —" Kara began.

"Then take this sauce." Eileen looked through the refrigerator and pulled out a big jar. "It's my special recipe, and it goes fine when you just boil 'em." Boiling obviously wasn't Eileen's idea of how to cook shrimp.

"I'm sure it does. Thanks a lot," Kara said, managing to make her way toward the car.

"Now you come back soon, you hear?" Kyle ordered in his friendly southern way.

"I'll do that."

It was dark when Kara got back to the houseboat. The night didn't seem nearly as friendly to her as Eileen and Kyle did. Being a city girl, Kara knew that just getting used to the place was going to take some doing. But if this was to be her temporary home, she'd have to learn jungle survival.

After boiling the shrimp, opening a container of potato salad and pouring a glass of wine, Kara went out to eat on the deck. The sky had just begun to darken. She dipped the sweet, tender shrimp in Eileen's sauce — which was delicious — and watched two large egrets stalk the shoreline for fish.

It was fine until night suddenly descended, swiftly, dark, and with a great deal of accompanying noise. There was splashing in the thick, slow-moving river; growling and mewling from the heavy undergrowth of shrubs that hugged the bank; and the flapping of wings overhead. All were ominous and threatening to Kara's ears.

She shivered and went inside. If she had to get used to her new home, she'd wait until daytime. She locked the door, turned on the air conditioner and left a light burning, so that when she climbed into bed she felt a little better. But there was no getting away from it: this *was* her home. At least for now. She couldn't sell the Sundowner without Nick's approval. At least not yet. She had no choice but to make it turn a big profit, and as Kara drifted to sleep she thought about how to achieve just that.

"Sean's little girl. Well, bless my soul. You're a sight for sore eyes." Buck, the relief bartender, greeted Kara as she walked into the Sundowner the next morning. He drew beers for the fishermen in the corner booth, then beamed at Kara. "Nick told me you were here." Reaching across the bar, he offered a huge hand for her to shake. "I'm pleased to meet you."

"It's nice to be welcomed for a change," Kara said, seating herself on a worn leather stool and glancing around apprehensively. There was no sign of Nick, and after her appointment with the accountant, she was relieved to be greeted with warmth and affection from the paunchy, gray-haired man behind the bar.

Buck frowned. "So Nick's been giving you a hard time?"

"He sure has," Kara said. She looked around again. Somehow, she could feel Nick's presence, but he wasn't there. "Arthur's not wild over me, either."

"Well, now, that'll change when you get used to each other," Buck said placatingly. "You've got to just give 'em a little time to cool down before they accept you."

"Yeah, about a thousand years."

"You got your daddy's spunk, that's for sure." Buck leaned companionably on the bar. "He was the greatest. I was in retirement after thirty years in the navy when I met him. Living on my pension but not happy. Bored? I tell you, I was bored to death. A widower with no kids. Lonely's what I was. Then Sean offered me this job. It was like a gift from heaven."

"I'm sure it was beneficial to Sean, too," Kara said. She didn't want to talk about her father now. She didn't want her mind going down the twisted path of her past with her father. Having begun to formulate a plan for the Sundowner, she didn't want distractions. She changed the subject, trying to sound casual as she asked her pointed question.

"What happens here at lunchtime?"

Buck laughed. "Place fills up with big eaters, that's what."

"Here in the bar?" She attempted to sound nonchalant.

"Sure. Right here. Our lunch crowd's mostly fishermen, and we have a lot of regulars who come in for the special. Some of 'em hang around in the afternoon to watch ball games on TV." He indicated a large screen in a corner of the bar. "Floridians are crazy about baseball. Do you know how many professional teams winter here?"

"Quite a few, I'm sure," Kara answered vaguely. "What about the dining room?"

"That gets busy at night with the overflow. Friday and Saturday the place is really jumping. We get a young crowd then. Nick's responsible for that. Once a month he books a local band and now and then some guy brings in one of those *Karaoke* machines so folks can sing along. They get up and carry on — make fools of themselves." Buck chuckled. "I've even performed a few times."

"What about daytime traffic in the dining room?" Kara persisted.

Buck made a thumbs-down gesture. "Empty as a tomb."

"But someone could get served there?"

"Well —"

"How about me?"

"You?" Buck echoed, his face crinkling in a big grin. "Honey, you're the boss. You can get served anywhere."

"Then I'd like to have an early lunch," Kara said, quickly glancing around once more, just to make sure Nick hadn't shown up.

"Go on in there and sit down. I'll send a waitress."

Kara had just settled into a chair at one of the dining-room tables when a soft voice said over her shoulder, "Miss Selwyn?"

She turned around.

"Buck sent me in to get your lunch order." Standing before Kara was a tall girl dressed in an outrageous costume consisting of a brief white skirt and a blue halter top with a wide white collar. Perched on her head was a ridiculous sailor cap.

The young woman raised one hand to straighten the cap self-consciously. "Our waitressing outfit. The customers love it."

"Well —" Kara began.

"I know. I didn't like it either when I first started working here but you can get used to anything, Miss Selwyn," she said with a shrug.

"You look lovely anyway," Kara said truthfully. The girl had managed to outshine her outfit. She was tall with thick brown hair pulled back in a ponytail. Her eyes were a deep golden brown that harmonized with her perfect tan. "And please call me Kara."

"I'm Melissa. Melissa Myers. And I want to tell you how much I miss your dad. He was the greatest."

"Thank you for those nice words."

"But it's true," Melissa went on. "He and Nick helped arrange my shifts so I could keep on at the community college. I never could have gotten that kind of flexibility anywhere else. So if I have to wear a silly outfit, it's a small price to pay."

Today seemed the day for fulsome praise of her father. And of Nick. She couldn't respond to the glowing words about her father, simply because she'd never really known him. But Nick was another matter. As far as Kara was concerned, he was a low-down snake. She certainly had no intention of listening to anything more about *him*.

"It seems strange that no one has lunch in here," Kara said, looking around the empty room. "No ladies' groups or mothers and children. None of the women who work in town or at the hotels along the beach. There aren't even any tourists here."

"I guess they think it's a man's world at noon," Melissa said with a laugh. "You know, good ol' boys swapping stories about the one that got away." Her comment was punctuated by a burst of male laughter from the bar. "But you're here," she said brightly, whipping out her pad. "What can I serve you?"

Kara perused the worn, flimsy menu. The offerings were a nutritionist's nightmare, the menu rife with fried foods — catfish, grouper, shrimp, and chicken. Hush puppies and french fries were offered as side dishes along with onion rings. Down at the bottom in tiny print was an announcement that some entrees could be broiled upon request, but Kara doubted if that option was encouraged or if any of the fishermen ever chose it.

"Um, the shrimp salad sounds awfully good —"

"Oh, we don't have that today," Melissa explained. "Arthur said he didn't feel like making it. But the fried shrimp roll is great," she advised.

"No salads?" Kara asked. They were the staple of her diet.

"Arthur doesn't like to make salads," Melissa explained. "He says coleslaw goes better with our menu."

"Hmm, interesting," Kara replied. "What about a shrimp cocktail?"

"That's on our dinner menu, but maybe I could ask him to fix it for you," she offered doubtfully.

"No, that's all right," Kara said hastily. "Just bring me the shrimp roll, coleslaw and a diet soda — if you have it," she added.

"We do," Melissa announced proudly. "And we have mineral water, too."

"A diet soda would be fine," Kara said absently. Her mind was preoccupied as Melissa disappeared into the kitchen with her order. It was time to get organized.

Last night Kara's head swum with ideas, nebulous as they were, which had taken form when she'd talked to the accountant this morning. It was time to record them. She pulled a spiral notebook from her purse, found a pen and began to write.

The dining room was hardly being used, not at all during lunchtime, and rarely at night except to accommodate the bar's overflow. Even a few customers would add to the profit; more than a few and it could be a gold mine.

Kara paused and looked around the room. Before she'd serve anyone a meal here, changes would have to be made. First, she'd begin with the decor. Get rid of the hideous oilcloth. Paint the old wooden chairs and tables bright colors. Hang plants from the beams. Bring in paintings for the bare walls. Surely there were artists in Cypress Key who'd like their work displayed. She jotted down the idea. Nick couldn't argue with a public relations move like that.

Nick. What would he have to say? She hadn't the slightest idea, but she was pretty sure he'd balk at her suggestions, if for no other reason than that they were hers. Well, she'd get her way in spite of Nick. She'd redesign, not only the offerings on the menu, but the menu itself. Make it brighter and easier to read. Forget the hackneyed nautical theme and come up with something sophisticated and tropical. Kara doodled a skinny palm tree in her notebook, wishing she had more artistic talent.

When Melissa reappeared with her lunch, she quickly put the notebook into her handbag. Before making any plans, she'd have to talk about them to Nick. Talk? That would be a change. Argue was more like it. Well, then they'd argue. She wasn't about to let him bully her. He had two choices at this point and both of them suited Kara: he could let her have her way or he could get out of the Sundowner. She much preferred the latter, but she'd settle for either one.

Kara ate her shrimp roll, which she had to admit was delectable, then went out on the deck and settled herself at a table shaded by a big umbrella. Topaz meandered out and plopped down beside her. Absentmindedly, Kara rubbed his back with her foot, and the old dog sighed with pleasure.

She leaned back, stretched and let herself enjoy the morning for a moment. The air was calm, the sky blue, the breeze gentle. Gulls and pelicans circled lazily above, now and then diving for fish beneath the surface of the placid Gulf. But her peacefulness couldn't last. If Topaz was here, she thought, Nick couldn't be far behind.

Still, there was no sign of him. There was, however, plenty of activity as the customers began to leave the bar. Just as Melissa had told her, they were mostly middle-aged men. They greeted her with a friendly hello before climbing down onto the dock and boarding their boats.

A few couples — retired, Kara judged — brought their coffee out onto the deck and sat for a while in the sun. No more than two dozen people had lunched at the Sundowner, and Kara meant to change that. It seemed so simple that she wondered why Nick and her father had never thought of it.

Well, she'd soon have a chance to ask Nick because he was charging up the steps from the parking lot. He looked like a boxer going after his opponent in the ring. There was just one problem: *she* was the opponent.

Topaz looked up, lazily swatted his tail against the deck and then fell back into his midday nap.

Nick strode straight to her and loomed over her. Kara tried to look as unconcerned as Topaz.

"Why the hell were you with my accountant this morning?"

Kara made a brief correction. "Not *your* accountant, *our* accountant." Then she smiled and said, "Good afternoon to you, too, Nick."

He had enough grace to look a little embarrassed but that didn't stop him from firing out a series of questions. "Why were you there? What's going on? How did you even know —"

"Tommy gave me the accountant's number and I made an appointment. It's as simple as that. I needed to get a grasp on how we're doing financially." Kara could see that her continual use of words like *ours* and *we* didn't please Nick. But that was just too bad. "We're doing pretty well. I was surprised."

Nick had settled down a little and was leaning against the railing of the deck. But Kara still envisioned him as a boxer, regaining his strength for a brief moment before going for the knockout.

He looked down at her with squinted eyes. She waited for him to speak. Finally, he said coolly. "I know how well the Sundowner is doing, Kara. I don't need you to tell me. In fact, I don't need you to do anything."

"You may not need me, but I'm here, and there's nothing either of us can do about it," she said flatly. "I also know what I'm doing, and I'm going to do a lot more." Why was it, she wondered, that his supreme self-confidence always managed to ignite her temper?

"Why were you in the bank? One of the tellers told me you were there."

"It should be obvious. I was signing bank cards, getting my name on the accounts and the checks. Doing everything a partner does," she explained.

"You should have asked me first." Nick folded his arms across his chest, a gesture that further irritated Kara, mostly because it accentuated his biceps and his broad chest in a distracting way. He could at least have dressed in a more businesslike manner, she thought, if he was going to the bank. Instead, he wore shorts, a tattered red T-shirt and thongs. Kara was dressed for success in a skirt and blouse. Why was it, then, that she felt at a disadvantage?

"I just brought along the appropriate documents proving I'm a partner. I didn't think I needed your permission," she said.

"Maybe not, but I don't like to find out from a bank teller what's going on at my own place."

"*Our* place," Kara emphasized. "Now if you'll be good enough to sit down, I'd like to discuss something with you."

Nick groaned, dropped into a chair and called out to Melissa, "Bring me a beer, please." Then he remarked to Kara, "I have an idea I'm not going to like this."

"Since you don't like anything about me, I wouldn't be surprised." Kara realized she wasn't helping the situation with her retorts, but they came unbidden. She drew a deep breath, reached into her purse and pulled out the notepad. "I have a plan."

"I'm sure you do."

Ignoring his comment, Kara continued. "I'm going to remodel the dining room."

Nick shot out of his seat. "No, you're not."

Kara was shocked by the sudden force of his disapproval. "Yes, I am," she threw back and stood up to face him.

"It's fine as it is."

"It's — it's tacky," she contradicted.

"That's your opinion."

"Ask anyone," Kara challenged.

At that moment, Melissa arrived with Nick's beer and gingerly put it down on the table.

"Thank you," Kara said, since Nick was obviously quite distracted.

"No problem," Melissa replied, scurrying away.

Nick's attention was focused on Kara; he didn't even notice that the beer had arrived. "The dining room's full every night," he said.

"And empty at lunchtime."

"That has nothing to do with the way it looks," Nick responded.

"Of course it does."

"No, it doesn't," Nick replied through clenched teeth.

"Yes, it does."

"Then why is the bar packed?"

"Because the old geezers don't care about their surroundings," Kara shot back.

"Right," Nick said. "They come for the food."

"No, they don't."

"Yes, they do."

"No, they —" Suddenly, Kara realized what they were doing. Here they were, face-to-face, practically screaming at each other over the lack of charm in the Sundowner dining room. It was ridiculous. She sat down. Nick slowly returned to his chair.

"I don't want to argue with you, but please listen to me," she said, keeping her voice low. She took a deep breath. "The lunchtime crowd comes to the bar because it's familiar and the food's agreeable. But there's another crowd that would pack the dining room if it looked pretty and had a more appealing menu."

"And who is this crowd?" Nick asked politely.

"The ladies who lunch. Tourists. Families. All we need to attract them is a new menu and a new look."

"Are you crazy?"

Lacking the energy to begin the whole argument over, Kara remained silent.

"No, let me rephrase that. You *are* crazy. You think after twenty-four hours you can waltz in and change the whole damned place. . . ."

Kara sighed. "No, just the dining room."

Nick jumped to his feet again. "Never!"

"Nick, please, just stay in one place and give me a chance to explain. I feel like we're a couple of jumping jacks — up and down, up and down —"

Nick inhaled a deep breath and settled back down in his seat. He took a gulp of beer. "All right. I'm willing to listen calmly, if it's possible to be calm around you. But just remember that you told me you didn't want to change anything, you just wanted to observe."

Kara nodded. "I did say that. But that was yesterday before I got my brainstorm. And remember, I did ask to see the books."

"And you could have — with me. But you had to do it alone. You had to take over."

"I didn't mean to 'take over'," she said, a little meekly.

"Well, that's what you seem to be doing. Hell, Kara, the books don't matter. This place does. The Sundowner has been fine the way it is for years. Can't you just let it be?"

"No," she answered adamantly. "I own half the Sundowner, Nick. I have the legal right to do what I please. I suppose we could go to court, but legal fees would cost you twice as much as what I plan to spend. Here —" she thrust the notebook at him "— look at these figures. Look at my ideas."

Grudgingly, Nick took the notebook and gave it a cursory look. "The figures are too low," he said. "You could never remodel for this amount."

"I'll do most of the work myself, on Mondays when we're closed and during the day. No one is in the dining room anyway. After I open for lunch, I'll get the remodeling expenses back in a month, I guarantee." Kara wasn't so sure about that, but it sounded good.

Nick was momentarily silent. Then his eyes brightened in challenge. "Arthur will never go along with this. He'll hate the menu, light cuisine, salads and sandwiches with cutesy names. Never in a million years."

"Leave Arthur to me," she said. Kara wouldn't admit it, but Nick could be right. Arthur was a potential obstacle, one she'd deal with when the time came. Right now, Nick was the problem.

"I don't approve," he said gruffly. "But you're going to do it anyway, aren't you?"

"Unless you physically restrain me," she challenged.

The look on Nick's face changed. His eyes,

which had been bright with anger through their encounter, narrowed slyly. His mouth turned upward in a sensual smile. Even the texture of his voice changed, becoming lower and more suggestive. "Now that might be an idea, getting physical . . ."

"No, I said —"

"I heard you, Kara. Maybe a physical encounter is just what we need at this point." He covered her hand with his and smiled at her. "It couldn't hurt. Maybe it could help." He ran his hand up her arm, slowly, but boldly. Nothing about Nick was tentative.

"No," she said. "No way, no time." She moved her hand away. Somehow he managed to turn every encounter into some kind of sexual contest. He made her uneasy, unsure. And Kara didn't like these feelings. The best way to handle them was to ignore them — and him.

"I'll begin the work tomorrow," she said brusquely. "And I think you'll be very surprised."

"Whatever you say," Nick muttered, turning away. "Come on, Topaz, I need a walk."

Reluctantly, the dog got up and with an apologetic look at Kara followed Nick down toward the beach.

Kara wondered if she'd develop a permanent back injury from all the painting she'd been doing. Gingerly, she got to her feet and stretched. Three days of nonstop work had made a difference in the dining room. At least she thought so.

Nick was of another mind. He'd been distant and disinterested as had most of the staff. But Melissa had joined in to paint in her spare time. And Buck had helped hang baskets of impatiens and philodendron from hooks in the ceiling beams. The plants alone gave the room more appeal.

Now she was putting the final touches on the tables and chairs, painting them in radiant Caribbean colors — turquoise and fuchsia, lilac and parrot green. She planned to add bright napkins, centerpieces on the tables and a redesigned menu to give the guests the feeling they were on a tropical island. At least that was the effect Kara hoped for.

Leaning against the wall, she wondered what to do next.

"It does look nice."

Stunned, Kara turned to see Arthur, spotless in his white uniform, observing the room.

"Thank you," she managed to get out. Arthur, too, had been notably absent from the dining room for the past three days.

"Reminds me of home," he said softly. "The pretty colors, the plants —"

Kara breathed a long sigh of relief. "That's what I was hoping for, Arthur. An island touch."

"You gonna add a steel band?"

"Why, no . . . I hadn't . . ." Then Kara realized he was joking. "No, the sound of our jukebox from the bar will have to do, but maybe you can give me some other ideas."

Arthur took a seat on one of the fuchsia chairs and contemplated the ceiling. "You talking about the menu?" he asked finally.

"I guess I am," Kara admitted.

"Well, I'm not gonna dream up any island fantasies for you there. No Grand Bahama sandwich and no Barbados salad. My menu stays the same."

Kara realized immediately what she was up against, and inwardly resolved not to be intimidated by her employee. She had a lot at stake here; it was time to let her chef know it.

"I'm going to open the dining room for lunch, Arthur," she said firmly. "In order to attract the clientele I want, we're going to have to add to our menu."

He was stoically silent.

Undaunted, Kara continued, "If you don't cook for me, then I'm going to have to hire someone as my assistant to make sandwiches and salads. Of course, that person would be taking up space in your kitchen —"

"Blackmail, eh?" Arthur questioned.

"You might call it that. I call it logic, making this work for both of us."

Kara remained standing, and Arthur finally got up to face her. She was pleased that the look on his face wasn't entirely unfriendly.

"Your daddy was awful good to me, so I

74

guess I owe the family."

Kara nodded silently.

"Okay," he said. "You can hire someone to work a few hours a day in my kitchen, making your ladies' food — if he knows his stuff. I'll keep on with my menus, but now and then, if you're lucky, maybe I'll make a shrimp salad for you."

To Kara, that was a triumph. "Oh, thank you, Arthur. That's great."

"Now don't go getting all excited. Stop a minute and think about it. I'm going along with you because I don't think this lunchtime project will last. I feel I can afford to be generous. For a while anyway."

"A while is all I ask," Kara responded as Arthur walked away. She wasn't going to let his pessimistic words get her down. Instead, she was going to prove to both him and Nick that they were wrong about her scheme. Somehow the sight of Arthur's retreating figure gave her confidence. She decided against pointing out to him that his white uniform was now imprinted with the fuchsia paint from one of her bentwood chairs. He'd find out about it soon enough from the kitchen staff. Meanwhile, Kara managed to stifle a giggle as she watched Arthur push through the swinging double doors.

5

"I can't believe you've had so much experience," Kara said to the woman sitting across from her. "You're just who I need."

"Then we're both in luck," Betty Jacobs replied with a musical laugh. She had the exotic look of the Caribbean combined with the fashionable style of Europe.

Kara nodded in agreement. After interviewing half a dozen unlikely candidates for the job as her assistant, she'd found in Betty the perfect employee to help get the Sundowner into shape. In her late thirties, she was tall and slender with dark luminous eyes and the slightest trace of a foreign accent. Her experience was complemented by a wonderful kind of savvy.

"You've worked all over the United States and in the Caribbean, too, I see," Kara added, scanning her eyes over Betty's résumé.

"I'm well traveled," Betty replied.

One thing worried Kara about that. If she'd worked in so many exciting locales, what was she doing applying for this job? Kara frowned, perused the résumé again and then looked across at Betty. Her dark hair was pulled back from her face in a stylish knot. Her dress was smartly casual and accented with bold accessories that only a woman with her style could pull off — carved combs, earrings and bracelets in vivid colors.

The question had to be asked, so Kara decided to come right out with it. "Why in the world do you want to work at the Sundowner?"

Betty's melodious laugh rang out again. "I prefer the west coast of Florida to any place I've traveled. I particularly like Cypress Key and, if you must know, there aren't that many jobs available."

"You've been a hostess in restaurants and hotels —"

"Yes."

"A chef —"

"A sous-chef, actually. I never attended cooking school. And all my jobs weren't all that prestigious as you can see from the résumé. I've also been a waitress and a bartender."

"In very exotic places," Kara couldn't help emphasizing.

"I prefer it here for personal reasons."

"Family?" Kara asked.

"You might say so."

Betty smiled quixotically, and Kara decided not to question her further. That was her business. Kara's business was to find the best person for the job. That was certainly Betty.

"You're hired," Kara said. "When can you start? Today's not too soon for me."

"I like your enthusiasm. You're like your father in that way —"

"You knew Sean, too?"

"Everyone on this coast knew Sean," Betty said easily. "And to answer your other question, I can start right away. If you'll let me see your menu, I'll plan what to order and when."

Kara handed over the list she'd prepared.

Betty scanned it quickly. "Looks appealing. I can make the sandwiches and salads, of course. And we can discuss how you'd like these other items prepared."

"I'm sure you know better than I," Kara admitted. "I'll be able to hostess and work the cash register. It's not exactly high tech so I think I can manage it. I'm going to hire a couple of waiters for the dining room." Then an idea occurred to her. "Men. Young men."

"Handsome young men?"

"Exactly," Kara agreed.

"In short, tight pants?" Betty's eyes twinkled.

"You're a woman after my own heart," she said. "And am I glad I found you." Then she remembered the least appealing part of hiring her new assistant. "Before we go over the menu in detail, you'd better meet the male contingent at the Sundowner, Nick and Arthur. If you knew Sean, you may have met Nick, but I doubt you know Arthur, our chef. He can be a little . . . well, a little cranky now and then."

Betty flashed her devastating smile. "Honey, there's not a man alive I can't handle."

Kara wished she had the same confidence when it came to Nick. "You're getting better by

78

the minute," she said. Just then a cacophony of barking reverberated from beneath the deck.

"It sounds like a dog's cornered something," Betty said.

"That must be Topaz." Kara stood up, puzzled. The old dog was usually too laid back to bark at anything.

"You want to go find out?" Betty asked.

"Maybe I should. If you don't mind putting off our meeting with the men —"

"Honey, there's not a man alive I can't put off 'til another time."

Kara laughed. "I like you more and more."

"You go on, see what's happening. I'll just look over this menu again."

"I'll be right back." Kara pulled off her shoes and ran down the steps to the beach below. The tide was low, and the wet sand was cool beneath her feet. She found Topaz under the pilings, poised in an angry stance. The fur on his back stood up straight, and his barking became more ferocious when Kara appeared.

"Quiet, boy," she said ineffectually, then grabbed hold of the dog's collar and peered into the darkness beneath the deck. The object of Topaz's fury looked like a big bundle of feathers. But when the mound of feathers stirred and flapped its wings, Kara realized it was some sort of huge bird.

She tried to drag Topaz away, but he planted his paws firmly in the sand and held fast. His barking became a low, menacing growl. "Oh, damn," she muttered, knowing she'd have to get Nick.

"Stay, Topaz," she ordered weakly. He was going to do whatever he chose, and her command had no effect. However, the dog seemed in no mood to venture closer. Clearly, his bark was worse than his bite. She'd have time to find Nick.

Kara ran up the stairs and into the bar where he was socializing with his fishermen pals.

"Sorry to bother you," she said, "but Topaz has something trapped under the deck —"

"Reckon it's another one of your pelicans," a red-faced fisherman intoned. "Well, get to it, son."

"It didn't look like a pelican," Kara said as she followed Nick across the bar, picturing the graceful birds she'd seen sailing through the blue Florida sky. "It was huge though, and —"

Nick ignored her as he grabbed a net propped against the bar, opened a drawer and found what looked like a pair of pliers. "Are you coming?" he asked.

"Of course."

"Then come on." He headed out the door with Kara following.

Topaz hadn't moved, but the bird — if that's what it was — flailed wildly.

"Good boy, Topaz. Now stay," Nick ordered. The dog sank into a low crouch, still not taking his eyes off the prey.

"What is it?" Kara asked. "What's the matter?"

"It's a pelican caught in fishing line," Nick replied. "The hook's probably in his wing."

"What are you doing?" Kara asked as he swung the net in a broad circle.

Nick answered sarcastically, "Thought I'd catch him in the net and maybe cook him for dinner."

"Nick!"

"For God's sake, Kara, what the hell do you think I'm doing?" Nick netted the bird which was struggling and emitting piteous shrieks. "Do you want to help or are you going to stand there and look horrified?"

Kara stepped forward. "Of course I'll help — if you tell me what to do," she snapped.

"Hold him steady while I find the hook."

The bird was still now, paralyzed by the trauma. Kara held on gingerly at first and then with a stronger grasp, one hand holding the body and the other securing the long bill.

Nick worked his hands through the feathers until he found the hook. "Here it is. In the wing," he said. "Hold steady," he told Kara as he clipped the curve of the hook and pulled it out. The bird gave a shudder and then quieted.

"I don't think the wing's infected, but I need to cut away all this line." He began snipping with the clippers and pulling off the yards of fishing line that entangled the bird. His hands were strong and deeply tanned with long fingers that worked gently and efficiently to free the pelican.

But now Kara found herself watching his face rather than his hands. She saw a look of deep concentration there. Gone was the sarcastic sneer he seemed to reserve especially for her. In its place was a tender look of concern. There was something humane and kind-hearted about this Nick, who seemed to care so deeply for a defenseless bird.

Her hands ached from holding onto the bird. As it gained freedom from the fishing line, her job became even more difficult, but she was determined not to let go.

"That's good," Nick said finally. Kara wasn't sure whether his words were for her or the pelican. "I think I've got it all."

Nick looked at Kara for the first time since he'd begun the rescue. "You can let go," he said. "Let's see if it can fly."

Nick stood up and carried the bird down to the water's edge with Kara and a very interested Topaz trailing along behind. There Nick pulled back the net and with a great effort tossed the pelican into the air.

At once the mighty wings spread out and began to flap. The bird rose, circled, and then headed skyward. Topaz, barking enthusiastically, splashed down the beach after it. Nick and Kara watched until the bird disappeared from view.

"Thank you," Kara said. "That was something."

"It happens a lot," Nick told her. "Pelicans

get tangled in fishing lines and lures. They're not all as lucky as our friend today. Infection sets in quickly, and they die. Or the hook catches them in the eye —"

"How terrible," Kara said, shuddering.

"A half-blind pelican can't compete for the fish with its healthy feathered friends."

The tide had turned, and the water lapped around their ankles.

"What can be done about it?" Kara asked.

"Not much. We try to educate the fishermen who come to the Sundowner about looking out for the pelicans — and the manatees, too. We lost a lot of them to boat propellers."

"I never thought about that," Kara admitted.

"Yeah. It's too bad. We need to be more careful. After all, it was their ocean first."

Kara looked at him quizzically with her head tilted to one side and a slight frown wrinkling her forehead.

"That's not very flattering," Nick said.

"What?"

"The way you're looking at me. Like I'm some sort of sea specimen. Without the feathers."

"Sorry. It's just that . . ." She still couldn't get her thoughts together. "I was surprised that you . . . that you seemed to care so much."

"About what?" His eyes shone intensely.

"About the pelican, of course." What else would she have meant, Kara wondered.

He dropped his gaze. "Surprised that I actually showed some kindness and decency? Would it have been more fitting if I'd hit the bird with a shovel?"

"No, of course not. I mean . . ." Her voice trailed off. She wasn't sure she liked seeing this vulnerable, human side of Nick. It interfered terribly with the image she'd established.

"Do you do this often — rescue them?" she asked for lack of anything else to say.

"Whenever possible," he responded.

"That's . . . that's —"

"What, Kara?" Nick moved closer, looking down at her. The air was hot and steamy with no trace of a sea breeze. Kara could see the perspiration forming along his hairline and feel the warmth of his breath against her skin.

"That's nice of you," she said at last.

He laughed. She tried to look away, but his eyes mesmerized her. Topaz had returned and lain down at their feet. Kara sensed the dog's presence more than she saw him. She *saw* nothing but Nick.

"I'm a nice guy," Nick said. He raised his hand and let it drift gently along her face. "You didn't know that, did you?"

Kara shook her head.

"You don't really know anything about me, Kara. But I know a lot about you. I know what you think of me, for instance."

"No, you don't, I —"

"Yes, I do."

"Well, I've told you. . . ."

"That doesn't count, Kara. What you say and what you think are often two different things."

She tried to come up with a quick retort, but the words caught in her throat. He was so close, too close. His hand touched her shoulder, then slid down her arm.

He whispered in a raspy voice. "Right now you're thinking that I'm not such a bad guy. You're wondering if you misjudged me. You're wondering if maybe we could be friends."

"Well —" She couldn't seem to complete a thought.

"You're wondering if we could be *more* than friends." His voice was hypnotizing.

"No, I'm not," Kara managed.

"Yes, you are."

They seemed to be forever denying each other's words. But now it was more dangerous than before. Now it concerned their feelings — about each other.

"You may even be wondering what it would be like if I kissed you."

Kara snapped herself into alertness. "I most certainly am not." She stepped away from him.

Unfortunately, moving back meant stepping deeper into the water, sinking deeper into the sand. Kara had no choice but to return to where Nick stood on the firmer sand.

Immediately he drew her into his arms and lowered his mouth to hers. The effect was electrifying.

The kiss hit Nick like a bolt of lightning. The

feel of her, the taste of her. All of his glib talk meant nothing. Now there was only Kara.

Her lips were soft and sweet beneath his. He felt the moistness of her mouth, the heat of her body, and the full swell of her breasts against him. His arms tightened around her. He was lost.

Kara could not find the will to fight. The moment Nick's tongue touched hers, she found herself opening up to him, kissing him back.

Neither of them noticed the water lapping at their ankles. Topaz rubbed against their legs and they remained oblivious. Wrapping one leg around hers, Nick pressed his hips to her body. They embraced each other in the shallow water as though clinging for their lives.

"No!" Kara burst out suddenly. She pulled away and planted her feet as firmly as she could in the unstable sand. "No," she repeated. "I don't want to kiss you." Even as she said the words, Kara realized that she'd waited far too long for such a vehement protest.

Nick shook his head and smiled. "Honey, you've already kissed me, and I think you enjoyed it as much as I did. In fact, you may have enjoyed it even more," he teased.

"You're awful, Nick Fleming," she flared back at him. "You took me by surprise, that's all." She moved farther away, her feet groping for more solid support. "I didn't have anywhere to escape to — except the ocean. And I'm not about to drown because of you."

He laughed.

"As for the kiss . . . well, I've known better," she added fiercely.

"Sure you have."

Kara was finally regaining her breath, and her heart had ceased its erratic pounding. She noticed that he was also breathing heavily. His face seemed flushed and hot, and not just from the afternoon heat. She took some satisfaction in that.

She headed away from the water toward the Sundowner, kicking up sand as she went. Topaz followed at her heels. "Anyway, that kiss was beside the point."

Nick followed her. "Beside the point?" He tried to grab her arm and stop her but missed.

"It meant nothing. It didn't matter."

"I thought it was pretty hot, Kara. In fact, you really surprised me. You're quite a kisser."

Kara stopped abruptly and the dog tripped over her feet. Her temper flared. "I'm not in the mood for your ratings, Nick. Not now, not ever. The only relationship we'll ever have," she added, wagging her finger in his grinning face, "is a business one. And that will continue only as long as you insist on hanging around."

"You're the one who's hanging around, Kara. I live here, remember?"

She turned away and continued to stamp through the sand.

"I'm here to stay," he added.

"Well, I have staying power too, Nick — *and*

imagination — which is more than some people have."

"Meaning?"

"Meaning some people can think only with their . . . with their bodies." She hadn't really meant to say that, Kara realized. It just came out.

"And you don't?"

"No," she said. "I think with my mind."

"And what were you thinking when you were kissing me?" he asked teasingly.

They reached the stairs leading up to the deck. Kara climbed up two steps and stopped to look down at him. "I hired a new assistant, and she's remarkable. Even you won't be able to find fault with her."

"Oh?"

"Well, maybe I'm wrong about that. You manage to find fault with everyone and everything. But she's an experienced cook, a very competent woman. She'll be able to handle the dining-room menu, do the shopping. . . ."

"And who is this paragon of virtue?" Nick asked.

"Her name is Betty Jacobs and —"

"Dammit!" Nick yelled. "You hired Betty Jacobs? Oh, Kara, I can't believe this."

Kara stepped up onto the third step to escape from the vehemence of his response. "What's the matter with that? She knew my father, and I assumed —"

"That she knew me?"

"Does she?" Kara asked a little meekly.

"Yes. And she knows Arthur, too."

"I didn't know that." Kara had a feeling something more was coming but wasn't quite sure what.

"Yep. She knows him all right. They used to be married."

"Oh, no," Kara groaned.

"Oh, yes."

"Well." Kara needed time to think.

Nick wasn't about to give it to her. "They were divorced a few years ago. It was pretty stormy, and she left town."

"Well," Kara repeated. "I'm sure that has nothing to do with the restaurant —"

"Of course it does, Kara."

"I doubt if she even knows Arthur's still here."

"Don't bet on it."

They walked up the stairs to the deck. Betty was nowhere to be seen.

"Well," Kara said for the third time. "She's gone. I'm sure she changed her mind when I told her Arthur was here. So you see, it's all right. I'll hire someone else and —"

"Is that her purse on the table, with the big flower on it?" Nick asked.

"Yes," Kara said softly.

"She's still here, and she's here for a reason. And it has nothing to do with making sand-wiches and salads."

"Nick, I hired the best person for the job. I

admit I was a little puzzled why someone with so much experience wanted to work here, but I decided it was none of my business. And it's still none of my business. She meets all my requirements."

"What are you saying, Kara?"

"Betty stays." Whether she'd actually meant to say that or not, Kara wasn't quite sure. It had all happened too fast. Now she was in a bind and she had no choice but to stick with her initial decision. "We'll work something out. They'll get along fine in the kitchen."

Nick looked doubtful. "You didn't see them together before. This place isn't big enough for the two of them. It wasn't then and it isn't now."

"I'm sure you're exaggerating, Nick."

"On the contrary. It wouldn't be possible to exaggerate the animosity between those two. What do you suppose her motives are in coming back?"

"I'm sure I have no idea," Kara said firmly, "except that she wants a job and I have a job for her." Kara collapsed in a deck chair and Nick stood over her.

"I don't believe I've ever seen stubbornness like this in my life. First you come in here and start making changes over everyone's objection —"

"Everyone being you and Arthur," Kara reminded him.

He ignored her comment. "Then you hire

Arthur's ex-wife to work beside him in the kitchen. And when you find out what you've done, you say, 'she stays' as if that's all there is to it. You're beyond belief."

"Maybe he'll be glad to see her back here," Kara suggested.

"Oh, sure. As glad as he'd be to see a great white shark in his clam chowder."

"Arthur doesn't make clam chowder, but I've got it on the menu, and Betty'll be making it," Kara told him.

"You know what I mean, Kara. Don't get smart with me."

"Don't you get smart with me," she shot back. "I hired the best person for the job. How did you expect me to know she'd been married to the chef?"

"You said you were suspicious. Maybe you could have asked her why she was here."

"I did. She said she liked the Gulf coast."

"And you accepted that?" Nick asked in disbelief.

"It would have been a little strange, don't you think, for me to ask all the applicants if they'd been married to the chef?" Kara was having trouble defending herself, and she knew it. "I'm sure once she realizes that no one wants her here she'll leave."

"You don't know Betty very well."

"He may be very glad to see her," Kara attempted again.

"You don't know Arthur very well."

91

"I'll explain the situation to them both separately. You'll see, Nick. It'll all work out," Kara tried.

"Sure. It'll all work out."

He'd hardly completed the sentence when they heard a terrible racket from the kitchen that sounded as if all the pots and pans had been swept up and dropped by a gust of wind.

Nick's face wore a look of superiority. "Sounds like Betty and Arthur are becoming reacquainted."

6

Nick and Kara headed for the kitchen. Kara was right behind him as they pushed through the swinging doors.

Betty and Arthur stood on opposite sides of the gleaming kitchen, a whole rack of pots and pans littering the floor between them. For a long moment the quartet stared at one another.

Betty broke the silence. "Arthur was so excited about seeing me that he knocked over a row of copper cookware," she explained before she turned to Nick with a wide grin. "Why, hello, Nick, honey. Come and give me a hug."

Nick picked his way through the debris and took her in his arms. "It's been a long time, Betty. You haven't changed a bit."

Kara cringed a little at his words, but they didn't seem to faze Betty. "Neither have you, honey. I'm sure glad to see you again."

As the two embraced, Kara dared to steal a look at Arthur's face. He seemed to be hiding behind a shield of wariness. His eyes were guarded and watchful, his mouth drawn into a straight hard line.

He moved and another pot from the displaced rack rattled to the floor. The others looked at him and waited for what was coming next. It was only a question, directed to Betty.

"So what are you doing here?" he asked, his resonant voice strangely discordant.

"Just starting a new job," she stated evasively.

"In Cypress Key?"

"Why, yes," she replied.

"Where?"

Nick and Kara watched and listened, pointedly silent.

"Here," Betty offered.

"Whaddya mean 'here'?"

"Here at the Sundowner," she said finally.

"Oh, no." Arthur's usually booming voice was barely audible.

"I sure am," Betty said. "Kara hired me as her assistant." Evidently, she was pleased with herself and wanted everyone — especially Arthur — to know it.

He looked from Betty to Kara, his flashing brown eyes demanding an explanation.

Suddenly Kara, too, felt defiant. "Betty was perfect for the job," she explained. "And I had no idea —"

"It won't work," Arthur said, his words directed to Nick this time. "It won't work at all. This kitchen isn't big enough for both of us. Cypress Key isn't big enough for both of us."

No one denied that.

"You've got to do something about this, Nick," he demanded. "Now."

Kara held her breath, waiting for Nick's response. She expected him to back his chef,

94

leaving her in the crossover between Arthur and Betty.

Nick, with all eyes on him, walked over to the refrigerator, opened the door and brought out a pitcher of iced tea. "Drink, anyone?"

In unison, they all shook their heads.

He sauntered to the cabinet, found a glass, poured the tea and took a big gulp.

Kara suspected Nick enjoyed being the center of attention. But she also knew that he was having trouble making up his mind.

"Nick —" she prodded, uneasy about saying anything more.

Nick looked at her steadily for a long moment. "The point is, Kara, that this isn't my problem."

It was Arthur who protested at that, but Nick lifted his hand, silencing him. "First of all, my policy is hands off Kara's little domain. If she fails, she fails on her own." He gave Arthur a level look. "I think we discussed that once before."

"And if I succeed?" Kara asked.

He evaded the question.

"I would think the same rules apply, success or failure," Kara reminded him.

"Like I said, I have nothing to do with this, and neither does Arthur."

"But this woman —" Arthur gestured at Betty with a wooden cooking spoon "— is going to invade my kitchen."

"That's right. It's your kitchen," Nick agreed.

"We need to make that perfectly clear. Arthur works here full-time. As I understand it, you'll be part-time, Betty."

"I sure will," Betty said. "And I'll have nothing to do with any of Arthur's menus — they'll be his domain. I'll buy and prepare my own food. We can even put up a partition," she added airily, "so we don't have to see each other. After all, this is a job that I need badly."

Nick jumped on that. "I'd think you could work anywhere you wanted."

"Kara hired me, didn't you, Kara?" Betty asked, evading Nick's question.

"Yes, I did," Kara said, remembering her excitement when she'd interviewed Betty. She marveled at how quickly that enthusiasm had been shattered.

"So, there," Betty exclaimed.

"There's no contract," Arthur surmised.

"Not yet," Kara admitted.

"Well, then. . . ." Arthur looked at Nick who looked at Kara who looked back at Betty, hopelessly.

Betty was up for the challenge, Kara realized.

"I'm not the kind of person who lodges complaints about being given a job and then being fired the same day because of personal differences that are beyond my control."

"No, I'm sure you're not," Kara said. "Are you?"

"Well, Kara, I *was* promised the job."

"There's no contract," Arthur offered again.

"So what do we do?" Betty asked.

Nick finished his tea and went to the door, ready to make his exit. "As I see it, we can insist that Betty be . . . uh, terminated, which might cause her to complain to —"

"The Chamber of Commerce," Betty supplied. "Or the Florida Department of Job Services, or the Equal Opportunity —"

"Fine. Go ahead and complain," Arthur said.

"No." Kara and Nick spoke in unison.

Then suddenly Nick laughed. "That's the first time we've agreed about anything since you got to the Sundowner."

"It had to happen," Betty said jovially.

"We don't want to cause bad feelings," Nick said with a stern look at Arthur, "so let's work out a compromise."

"Just what would that be?" Arthur asked.

"A trial period once the dining room is open for lunch, of, say, two weeks."

"Two weeks!"

"It's not a lifetime, Arthur," Betty said.

"Two days'll seem like a lifetime with you in my kitchen," Arthur countered.

"Two weeks with Arthur running the kitchen, and Betty working for Kara." Nick looked at Arthur. "You can do it."

Arthur grunted in response. "Well, maybe in two weeks, lunchtime in the 'Caribbean Room' will be only a memory."

Kara kept her mouth shut. Now wasn't the time to argue with Arthur.

"All right," Arthur said. "I'll agree, if this woman —" he pointed the spoon at Betty "— promises not to mess with my kitchen and if she stays out of my way. She can work back there." He indicated a table in the rear of the room. "But she can't use my refrigerator. I mean that. Give her one rack and she'll take over the whole thing."

"Is there another refrigerator?" Kara asked Nick.

"Sure. The one we store beer in. She can have a rack in it."

"Give her a rack and she'll take —"

"Arthur —" Nick warned.

Kara continued. "I'll get a grill for cooking, or whatever Betty needs. We'll be totally autonomous. You'll see, Arthur. Just like they say on the islands — no problem."

Nick grinned. "Now that that's solved. . . ." With those words, he pushed through the swinging doors and was gone.

Kara wasn't sure anything was solved, but at least she had a temporary truce. Maybe somehow it would enable her to get her dining room plans off the ground. "Well," she said. "Everything seems to be working out."

"You haven't asked me how I feel about this, Kara," Betty said.

"Why, no. I guess I haven't." Here it comes, she thought, World War III.

Betty broke into a big smile. "It's wonderful! I can't wait to be back working at the

Sundowner. And Arthur, honey, don't you worry. I'm going to do just what you want me to. It'll be just like the old days."

Kara groaned inwardly and glanced at Arthur. He was still holding the spoon, like some kind of weapon.

"Only better," Betty continued, " 'cause you and I won't even see each other."

"How do you figure that?" Arthur seemed to choose his words carefully.

"We'll put up a partition."

"I don't think that'll be necessary, just for two weeks. We can ignore each other."

"Each of us pretend the other doesn't exist?" Betty asked.

"No. I mean yes."

Clearly, Kara thought, Arthur wasn't sure *what* he meant.

"Fine," Betty said. "You go your way and I'll go mine."

"Oh," Arthur said. Then he added quickly, "Fine."

"Now I guess it's time for me to get back to the menu," Betty said. With a swing of her hips she strolled out of the kitchen, leaving Kara and Arthur to share an uneasy silence.

Several days later, the Sundowner dining room had its grand-opening for a catered luncheon. At the end of the day, Betty found Kara on the deck, collapsed in a chair like a rag doll.

"You survived," Betty said.

"But barely," Kara replied dully, her eyes focused on the floor.

Betty placed a reassuring hand on Kara's shoulder. "Considering it was the first time, things went as well as could be expected."

Kara finally raised her head and heaved a sigh. "By that do you mean getting the orders confused and spilling tea on the luncheon's hostess and —"

"And listening to an irate patron's tirade about the poor choice of putting pecans in the chicken salad." Betty sank into a chair beside Kara.

"How was I to know the woman couldn't eat nuts?"

"I guess in any large group of women, you're bound to find at least one with digestive problems. Especially among a group called the Over Sixty and Proud of It Birthday Club," Betty said.

Kara smiled wanly. "Whose idea was it to add the pecans, anyway?"

"Yours," Betty replied.

"Oh. Well, I made a mistake. But it was a delicious salad. Everyone else liked it."

"They sure did," Betty agreed.

Kara stared out over the Gulf and mused, "Maybe I shouldn't have started off with a catered luncheon for thirty women. Maybe I should have just quietly opened for lunch two or three times a week to see what would happen."

"Nonsense. It was baptism by fire which is the best way, believe me. Just get out there and *do* it. I've faced those choices a few times," she added with a chuckle. "And the timing was perfect — a Monday when the Sundowner is normally closed. No men around to butt in and give advice. It was fine, and it'll get better, Kara."

"I hope so. It was just so embarrassing and confusing when I couldn't remember who had the shrimp salad and who had the chicken and who wanted diet dressing and who . . . Well, there's no need to rehash it. You were a witness."

Betty chuckled again. "Let's just say you're not cut out to be a waitress."

"That's an understatement. I wonder if I'm even cut out to manage the new dining room."

Betty leaned forward and looked directly at Kara. "Of course you are. The luncheon was very well planned. When business picks up, you can hire waiters and someone to work the cash register, which you did quite well, by the way."

Kara had already put the day's earnings in an envelope, which she held on to protectively. "Yes, we made a nice profit, even after subtracting the cost of cleaning Mrs. Perry's dress."

"I'm sure it was only a little spill."

"And it wasn't hot coffee, only iced tea. And it didn't land right in her lap — it only dribbled down her bosom."

They both laughed. "It's all part of the game," Betty said as she stretched her arms over her head. "Now, unless you need me, I'm going home to take a nice cool shower."

Kara glanced at her watch. "It's almost six o'clock. You've put in a full day, Betty. Thanks for staying to help clean up. I had no idea it would take so long."

"I know how Arthur likes his kitchen, and if it wasn't spotless, we'd never hear the end of it."

"You and Arthur . . ." Kara began tentatively. "Is it working out in the kitchen? Please," she begged, "I need good news."

"It's going fine, honey. As long as I don't tell him how to fry up the seafood, and he doesn't tell me what kind of greens to put in the salad, we get along great. Arthur can be a very charming man when he wants to."

"He's certainly a very attractive one."

"That he is," Betty agreed with a sigh. "I'd almost forgotten how attractive. And he seems more laid back now."

"Laid back? Arthur?"

"In the old days we couldn't be in the kitchen two minutes without a fight. I'd say rosemary. He'd say thyme. Arguing with Arthur over spices seems kind of silly now. There're other ways to get his attention."

Kara narrowed her eyes. "Betty, are you and Arthur . . . I mean, you're divorced, and you seemed . . ."

"We had some bad times, but we had good times, too. Right now, it's strictly business."

"Hmm. Is that why he made the salad for us?"

Betty just grinned. "That's all I'm saying about Arthur for now. It's time to head on home. You've worked nonstop getting the place ready and putting out the word we're open for business." She gave Kara's arm a pat. "You're a marketing whiz, not to mention a first-class decorator. Plenty of hard work led up to today."

Kara leaned back in her chair and smiled. "Yep, they know we're here, and it does look classy, doesn't it?"

Betty looked across the porch into the brightly decorated dining room. "And a thousand light-years away from the shabby place it used to be. We're just starting to roll. I predict you'll be as successful as Nick has been."

"Nick?"

"He is successful, Kara, even though his taste in decor is abominable. He knows how to keep the customers coming in — he and Arthur," she amended.

Grudgingly, Kara had to admit that Betty was right. Nick had a magic touch with the bar. "There's more than one way to run the Sundowner, though," she added.

"You don't have to prove it all in one day. Now, close up and go on home," Betty ordered.

"In a minute, I just want to check a few more details —"

"Well, I've had it." Betty got to her feet. "See you tomorrow."

"Good night, Betty, and thanks. I never could have —"

"Done it without me." Betty flashed a smile. "I know."

Kara spent another half hour in the dining room going over luncheon receipts. She was only two dollars off, which she considered a minor miracle when she thought of the nightmare of making change for thirty people. But she'd survived, and some of the women had talked about coming back when the Sundowner opened for lunch on a daily basis.

Still, she hadn't imagined how grueling restaurant work could be, both physically and emotionally. She and Betty had been in the kitchen since eight that morning. To Kara's amazement, Arthur had left a huge bowl of shrimp salad on Betty's rack in the refrigerator. Betty had just smiled mysteriously about Arthur's donation and instructed Kara to start chopping.

She'd cut up chicken breasts, diced celery and onions, sliced tomatoes and avocados, and shredded the lettuce. Then she'd set the tables, greeted the guests, taken orders, served the food, filled glasses, poured coffee and brought out the birthday cake Betty had baked.

Thank God Nick hadn't been there to watch her running around like Topaz chasing a sea gull. Thank God he hadn't seen her spill the tea on Mrs. Perry. Thank God. . . .

"Who cares what Nick Fleming thinks about anything?" Kara asked herself aloud. "Who the hell cares?"

She left the dining room with the envelope in her handbag. She'd stop at the night deposit on the way home. Then she'd follow Betty's advice and pamper herself with a cool shower and a glass of wine before settling down for a long night's sleep.

Kara locked the dining room door behind her and paused a moment on the deck. The sky was streaked with hues of orange, rose and fuchsia emanating from the red ball of the sun that hovered on the water's edge.

"Wow," she breathed as she stood at the rail, drinking in the spectacle. She made a mental note to take a few minutes every day to watch the sunset over the Gulf.

"It's free, and it's the best show on the coast."

Startled, Kara turned at the sound of Nick's voice.

He slowly ascended the steps and stood beside her at the rail. He was barefoot, wearing only a pair of shorts.

"I didn't hear you," she said accusingly.

"I came up from the beach. Been fishing with some guys on the other side of the point."

"Catch anything?" she asked, trying to avoid looking at his broad, sun-bronzed chest.

"Two good-size red snappers. They're on ice downstairs so Arthur can cook them up in the morning. Great for breakfast," he added. "Like to join me?"

"I'm not crazy about fish for breakfast."

"Have you ever tried it?"

"Well, actually —"

Nick laughed. "The offer still stands. So how'd the luncheon go?" His question was lazy and casual.

"Great. No problems," she lied.

"Good to hear that. You still think you can make a success of the place?"

"You'd better believe it," Kara replied with more fervor than she felt.

"I expect the locals are more tolerant since you're Sean's daughter."

Kara looked up sharply at Nick. His expression of studied indifference made her nervous. It didn't help that he was practically naked. Her gaze kept straying from his face. She noticed with fascination how the dark hair across his tanned chest narrowed to a thin line on his abdomen and disappeared into his shorts. Her eyes skimmed downward to his hard thighs and calves. She tingled with the remembrance of their kiss and the feel of his muscular body against hers.

Forcing her gaze back to his face, Kara responded. "What exactly do you mean by 'more tolerant'?"

"The tea on Mary Beth Perry's new silk dress."

"How did you know — ?"

"I was fishing with Ned Perry and stopped by his house for a beer after. Mary Beth filled me in on the luncheon."

Kara felt a sinking sensation in her stomach. "It was nothing, really," she said, pretending nonchalance. "Just one of those things that happens now and then." She paused before asking, "What did Mrs. Perry say?"

"She said you'd graciously offered to have the dress cleaned and since you were Sean's daughter and my partner, she wouldn't sue you."

Kara saw the hint of laughter in his eyes. "You're lying, Nick Fleming."

"About the lawsuit, yes. Not about her friendship with Sean and me. That's probably why she booked in the first place."

"Did you happen to ask how she liked the food and the decor, by any chance?"

"Actually, no," he replied.

"Thanks a lot. We own the Sundowner together, Nick. You could show a little interest."

"These women's luncheons weren't my idea, Kara."

"But they've happened. They're a fact. I should think as a partner you'd show some enthusiasm rather than treating me like a charity case."

"I didn't ask questions, Kara. I just listened, and what I heard is that everyone's curious about why you're still here."

"Well, ask Mary Beth Perry. I'm running a restaurant, and doing a good job," Kara said between clenched teeth.

"Since there already was a popular restaurant here, doing a good business, folks just figure there's more to it."

Kara looked right at him, ignoring the way the sunset created a golden glow on his bare skin. "Oh, do they?"

"Yeah, so I filled them in on the real reason you're hanging around Cypress Key."

Kara saw the wicked smile playing around his lips and kept her own mouth shut firmly.

"I told them the restaurant business was only secondary. The real reason you're here is because you're wild about me."

"You said that?" Kara's voice rose in dismay.

"It's the truth, isn't it?" Nick asked blandly, crossing his arms across his bare chest and grinning.

"Of course it's not," she shot back.

"Oh, sure it is, Kara. You just don't know it."

"I'm going to assume you're joking, Nick."

"Joking? Don't you remember our kiss — right down there on the beach?" He pointed toward the water. "Sparks from that kiss could have caught this old place on fire and burned it to the ground."

She looked out across the Gulf, trying to compose herself. "This isn't about kisses. It's about — oh, Nick, you confuse me so much, I don't know what it's about."

He gently ran the fingers of one hand up her arm. She felt a quiver begin at the nape of her neck and travel like lightning down her spine.

"Electricity, Kara. Us."

Kara felt as if everything had stopped — her breathing, the wind in the palms, the ebb of the water. Her eyes met Nick's; they were teasing, sexy and they held her with their power. One more moment close to him and she'd reach out and run her fingers along the smooth lines of his chest, one more moment. . . .

This wasn't supposed to be happening. She hated Nick. Didn't she?

Kara forced herself to pull away from his grasp. "Us?" she asked. "There is no us, Nick. There's you and there's me. And there's this sham of a partnership." She fought for control of her voice, cursing herself for being flustered and shaky just when she wanted to be cool and commanding.

Nick grinned cockily. "Everything between us is very real, Kara. Come on, let's go upstairs where it's nice and cool. We'll have a drink, talk things over —"

"The only thing I have to say to you is good night." Kara knew she had to get away, put distance between her and Nick before something dangerous happened. She grabbed her handbag and started across the deck, almost running.

Nick's voice floated lazily behind her on the

hot, tropical air. "Does this mean our breakfast date is off?"

Why, Kara wondered, did Nick always have the last word? On the drive back to the houseboat, she replayed that final scene. It was so like him to taunt her and keep her confused. Whenever she was around him, she felt off center.

There was so much Kara wished she'd said to Nick on the deck but — with him strutting around half-naked, touching her, talking about kisses — her mind had gone blank. Even now that she was away from him, she couldn't get Nick out of her head. *Sparks,* he'd said. *Electricity.* She could handle it, Kara told herself and then repeated aloud. "I can handle Nick Fleming."

But which Nick? The arrogant, macho man who tried to give her orders about the Sundowner, or the businessman respected by his staff and the community? The teasing Nick who seemed to delight in unnerving her, or the kind, gentle Nick who took care of wounded birds? Or, most confusing of all, the Nick who looked at her with such naked desire that she had to run away?

Damn him.

Finally she saw the little houseboat ahead, bobbing on the water, and gave a sigh of relief. Even if it wasn't exactly her dream home, at least it was some form of haven after a long day.

She'd lie down and try to clear her mind of any thoughts about Nick Fleming.

She opened the door and stepped inside, ready for the welcome rush of cool air. It didn't come. Instead, she was greeted by a heat so stifling it took her breath away. A steam bath would have been more refreshing. Kara was certain that she'd left the air conditioner running that morning, but maybe in her rush to get to the Sundowner, she'd forgotten.

She turned on the light and checked the controls. The knob pointed to ON. Frantically, she turned it off and then on again. There was no hum of response, no burst of coolness. The air conditioner was dead.

Muttering expletives under her breath, Kara flung open the windows and doors. It was hopeless. The air lay hot and heavy across the river, no breeze stirred in the humid night. Perspiration poured down her neck. Kara grabbed a towel and blotted it away. Then she examined the air conditioner again.

How like Nick Fleming to stick her with an old decrepit piece of equipment. He probably knew it would fail, she thought as she turned all the available knobs, plugged and unplugged the cord, and then banged on the machine with her fist.

Frustrated, Kara ripped off her clothes and jumped into the shower. She let the cold water splash over her until she felt reasonably chilled. Then she dried off and, still wrapped in the towel, poured herself a glass of lemonade. Curled up on the bed, she sipped her drink and immediately felt the heat encompass her again, worse than before. Somehow the momentary coolness made the heat even more oppressive.

She considered her options. Sleeping in the houseboat was impossible. She'd lie awake all night bathing in her own perspiration. Even less appealing was the thought of dragging her mattress onto the deck where mosquitoes would eat her alive. Hot and frustrated, she flopped back on the bed.

An image of Nick suddenly came into her mind. Nick, lolling about in the air-conditioned comfort of the apartment above the Sundowner. Her father's apartment, the rooms that should be hers! He'd sleep there comfortably tonight while she'd lie awake in a steam room praying for daylight. He'd probably listen to music, read, watch television, do all the things appropriate to a normal existence. She'd sit awake on a boat in a murky river, hoping for the slightest breeze to stir the tattered curtains. It was preposterous and she wouldn't stand for it, Kara decided suddenly.

She surged to her feet, determined that he wouldn't get away with it. He wouldn't stick her in a dilapidated boat in the middle of nowhere while he enjoyed the good life. No way.

Kara yanked open the drawer beside her bed,

pulled out a fresh pair of shorts, a T-shirt and underwear, and tugged them on. Then she grabbed her purse and slammed the door behind her.

She and Nick were long overdue for a showdown.

7

Kara pushed past Nick into the apartment, not noticing his surprise or registering his remarks. What did get her attention was the delightful chill of air conditioning.

"Kara, what in the world —"

She stopped in the middle of the room and looked out through the floor-to-ceiling window. "Nice view of the Gulf," she commented before turning to take in the rest of the apartment. It was large and airy with low-key but attractive furniture — a few pieces in pale oak, an over-stuffed sofa and a couple of comfortable-looking chairs. The walls were marine blue with white trim. "The colors are a little nautical for me," she said, "but it's certainly cool. Overall it'll do fine." At one end of the room she noticed a small kitchen and an open door that led into a bedroom. "Yes, this will do."

"Thanks for the decorating critique. Anything else on your mind?" Nick asked.

"There's a lot on my mind, Nick. Number one is that you're moving out," she announced, "and I'm moving in. You can pick up your clothes tomorrow."

"What the hell are you talking about? I'm not going anywhere." He was still barefoot, still wearing his khaki shorts. The muscles of his chest gleamed with a bronze sheen in the lamp-light.

"You might want to put on some clothes before you leave."

"I'm not leaving," Nick replied.

"I hate to disagree with you, but I'm taking over this apartment. If you want to know why, I'll be pleased to tell you. The air conditioner in the houseboat is dead. Kaput. Terminal. The place is like a sauna, and I'm not sleeping there. Tonight or any other night."

Nick nodded understandingly. "Yeah, it's a pretty old unit. I thought you might have to get it replaced sooner or later."

"*I* might have to?" she asked in amazement. "You installed it, and you can replace it. You own the boat —"

"And you're living in the place rent-free, Kara. You need to take some responsibility."

Nick's calm, reasonable tone did nothing to placate Kara. In fact, it only inflamed her more. "I *am* taking responsibility. I'm taking over the responsibility of my father's apartment. My *father's*," she repeated.

"And where do you suggest I sleep? Out on the beach?"

Kara could tell Nick wasn't taking her demands seriously. "Go to a motel. To Arthur's. To the Perrys' — I'm sure they'd love a chance to hear more of your stories about me. Go anywhere. Just leave, Nick. I'm tired. It's been a long day, and I'm ready for a good night's sleep."

Nick was silent for a long moment before taking a step toward her, slowly, calmly. "Now, Kara," he said, "you're overwrought and out of control. Let's have a cool drink and talk this over. I'll work everything out." The soothing tone of his voice did nothing to placate her.

"Work it out? The two of us will never work anything out, Nick. There's nothing more to be said."

"Kara —"

"Don't even try it, Nick," she warned. "I'm not in the mood. You've done all the damage you're going to do."

"What damage —"

"I'll tell you what," she shouted. "First you steal my father's apartment, stick me on a boat with a twenty-year-old air conditioner, and then you tell lies about me to the Perrys —"

"Kara, if that's it, I didn't tell them —"

"Don't bother to deny it, Nick. It doesn't matter anymore. Just get out. That's all I ask." She pointed toward the door. "I've had it with you."

Nick shrugged, turned away and sat down in one of the comfortable chairs Kara had coveted from the moment she'd walked into the apartment.

"There's no way I'm leaving," he told her. "I don't know what this is all about, but if you're uncomfortable on the boat and want to spend the night here, be my guest. But I'm not giving up my bed. Not even for you, Kara."

"I want this place, and I want it now, Nick." Kara realized that she was being irrational, she wanted to stop her tirade, but she couldn't. The stream of emotion that had washed over her on the houseboat had become a tidal wave. For once, she was going to have the last word.

"Kara, you're talking like a crazy person," Nick warned.

"If I'm crazy, it's because you've made me this way. We've reached a showdown, and it's been a long time coming." Kara realized that her hysteria was building, but she did nothing to stop it. Maybe this was the only way to handle the turmoil inside her. "I'm finally saying exactly what I think, and if you can't take it, then get out. In fact, whether you can take it or not, leave. Just leave!" she shouted.

"Kara, come over here and sit down," Nick attempted again. He motioned to the chair beside his. "I'll get you a glass of wine, and we can relax and discuss this like civilized people."

"Don't patronize me, Nick. I'm perfectly civilized, and I don't care to be treated as if I were a hysterical child."

"Act like one, and I'll treat you like one."

"Don't you dare —"

"Kara, I've had just about enough of this. Grow up or go home."

"I'm not about to go back to that steam room."

"Then go back to Atlanta," he shouted.

"Never!"

Nick stood up and took a step toward her. "Then sit down and cool off." He reached out, and reacting instinctively, Kara raised her arm in a gesture of self-protection.

"For God's sake, Kara, I'm not going to hit you."

"How do I know that?" she asked, her voice high-pitched.

"Kara —" He reached out again.

Quickly, she stepped back and picked up a vase from the end table, lifting it in both hands and aiming it directly at Nick's head.

"Don't touch me, Nick. I've had it with you!"

"You *are* crazy." Before she could react, he caught her arm and wrestled the vase from her hands.

After placing the vase on the floor out of her reach, he returned and grabbed her by the shoulders before she had a chance to move. "You could have killed me."

"That was the idea," Kara said, squirming in his grasp, flailing at him as she tried to break away.

Nick pulled her close and wrapped his arms tightly around her. "Kara, you have the wrong idea about me. I'm not the enemy —"

"If you aren't, who is?" she asked.

"Maybe you're your own enemy."

"That's ridiculous," she cried as she attempted to stamp on his bare foot.

He lifted her until her feet skimmed the floor. "I don't think so."

She felt trapped, and that was enough to make her fight with renewed desperation. Ineffectually, she pushed against his shoulders with her hands. Her palms were damp and sweaty and slid over his skin like satin. Somehow their confrontation had turned into an erotic contest. Kara tried to block out the sudden awareness that he'd become aroused. But it was impossible to ignore the sensual pressure of his lower body against her.

She was beyond desperation now. "Let me go!"

"Never," he responded.

Kara aimed a kick at his calf and smiled in satisfaction when Nick grunted and loosened his hold.

In an instant Kara slipped away from him and sprinted toward the bedroom door. If she could get inside and lock herself in, then the room would be hers. Possession was nine-tenths of the law, Nick had said. Now Kara would use those words against him.

He was right behind her. She shut the door but not quickly enough. He threw his weight against it and the door flew backward, propelling Kara across the room and onto the bed. Nick's momentum flung him on top of her.

For a moment, Kara's breath was knocked out of her. Then she began to struggle against Nick's weight. "Get up, you fool," she cried. "Get off me."

"Not until you stop acting like a crazy

woman." His quick, shallow breathing matched hers. She could hear his heart pounding as he lay on top of her. "What the hell is it, Kara, what's happening to you?"

"It's not me, it's you! You're ruining my life. Telling people I'm wild over you, telling them you're the reason I'm still here. . . ."

Nick raised his head and looked down at her. His eyes glowed in the low light of the bedroom lamp. "I never told anyone that, Kara."

"You said —"

"But you must know I was teasing."

"Then why —"

"Because it's true." His voice was low and husky. "I didn't tell anyone, but I'm telling you," he said. "What's between us is the reason that both of us are here. Now. Like this. Isn't it, Kara?"

She couldn't answer. She felt as though her lungs would burst from lack of oxygen. She wanted to scream out and tell him this was all wrong, it wasn't what she wanted. But that would be a lie. From the moment he'd kissed her on the beach, this had been exactly what she'd wanted. He made her crazy. He drove her to distraction. He was the most exciting man she'd ever known.

"Kara —" He touched one hand to her face.

She couldn't even speak his name. All she could do was feel. Feel his body against hers, the sensual curve of his mouth so close, the coolness of his breath on her face, the touch of his fingertips along her cheek and across her mouth. The sensations unleashed all the emotions she'd fought so hard to hold in check. Slipping her arms around his back, she took the tip of his finger into her mouth and tasted the saltiness of his skin with her tongue.

When she saw the look of longing and desire that had transformed his expression, she allowed her body to fully respond to his. Nick's bare chest pressed against her and she could feel her nipples tingle and harden under her shirt. Nick's eyes told her that he knew very well how her body was reacting. He gave a low satisfied moan and, slipping his finger from her mouth, he lowered his lips to hers.

Kara closed her eyes, and Nick kissed her.

His tongue made a pleasurable invasion of her mouth. Kara could feel a slow, smoldering heat begin to grow deep inside her. Her body felt heavy and weak as if all her bones and sinews were melting under the heat of their embrace. It suffused her. It made her complete.

He kissed her neck, sliding his lips along her jaw bone to her ear. His breath, hot against her skin, sent little prickles of desire all along her nerve endings.

"I didn't tell the Perrys that you were staying here because of me," he murmured. "I lied, Kara. That was my own secret fantasy, hoping you wanted me the way I wanted you."

She knew that. She'd known it all along, but it touched her deeply to hear him say it. The fantasy of their mutual desire had become reality. She gave herself to it.

Nick's tongue made forays of discovery inside the shell of her ear. Tensing, Kara tightened her arms around his back. His skin was moist and pliable against her hands. Then one of his legs insinuated itself between hers and he was all heat and muscle against her.

Her heart pounded out of control and her breath quickened as if she'd been running for miles.

Nick's mouth found hers again, and their kiss was long, thorough and deep. This time she explored him with her tongue, tasting him, drawing him into her mouth. It was an irrational fantasy, and she didn't want it to stop.

Nick moved his hand inside her shirt and fumbled for the hook of her bra. When it released, he cupped her breast, rubbing his palm against her nipple until Kara felt an aching need spiral through her.

"Oh, Kara," he whispered, "you feel so good. So good." He pulled her shirt over her head, then tossed the scrap of bra on the floor. "I want to see all of you, touch all of you." His mouth moved to her breast, and Kara moaned in pleasure as he drew her firm nipple into his mouth. She wrapped her fingers in Nick's thick, dark hair and pulled him closer.

He tugged off her shorts and ran his hand up the sensitive skin of her inner thigh. "I knew you'd have great thighs," he murmured hoarsely. Then he found the edge of her panties and slipped them off. She was moist and warm, and his fingers caressed her until she cried aloud with need. The tension inside coiled and tightened, sending waves of pleasure mixed with longing through her body. She experienced a desire for him that couldn't be denied, a need that had to be fulfilled.

"Can you feel how good we are together, Kara?" he whispered. "I know it could get even better. I want to show you, I want . . ."

Kara had no voice to answer. With trembling hands, she struggled to undo the zipper of his shorts. Finally she managed to say, "Help me, Nick."

He worked his way out of the shorts, kicked them to the floor and then took Kara's hands in his. "Touch me, Kara. Touch me, please."

She put her hand where he wanted it most, and as she caressed him, she felt him grow harder in her hand.

"Oh, Kara. What you do to me. You make me crazy."

Kara continued to stroke his erection as she lowered her head and touched each of his nipples with the tip of her tongue. She was wanton and wild, not like herself at all, and yet more like herself than she'd ever thought she could be.

She covered his mouth with hers for a long kiss, then pulled back. "You have a beautiful mouth," she whispered, not even aware that she was saying the words. "Even when I hated you, I noticed your mouth. I loved your mouth."

"And you have beautiful breasts." He kissed one, and then the other. "And beautiful skin." He ran his tongue lightly across her belly. "Even when I thought I hated you, I noticed your breasts and your skin," he said. "But I never imagined how beautiful you would be here." His lips found the moist softness between her legs. "I never knew how sweet it could be."

His tongue worked magic, transporting her out of herself until nothing remained but a sweeping desire that left her breathless. The tension was unbearable — she wanted to scream and cry out — but she was only able to whisper. "Oh, Nick, I want you so much. . . ."

Slowly, gently, he entered her. His heat and strength filled her, and she enveloped him in her soft warmth. She dug her fingers into the muscles of his back, as their bodies moved in harmony, locked in slow, perfect rhythm.

He paused their motion to smooth away a damp curl from her face. "Are you all right?" he whispered in a husky voice.

Kara smiled up at him, her eyes dreamy and faraway. "I'm more than all right. Oh, Nick, I'm in heaven."

"Me, too." His thrust deepened, his heart raced and his blood surged wildly.

Kara wrapped her legs around his and tilted her hips to fit their bodies even closer. They were lost in their lovemaking, each movement bringing them nearer and nearer to fulfillment. Then the moment arrived when together they knew that it could go on no longer.

It came with a shattering, blinding intensity that stopped time, crossed space, reached eternity. They clung to each other, hot and wet, united in a joy beyond anything either of them could have imagined.

"Nick," she murmured after a while. She didn't know how long. It didn't matter how long.

"I know," he whispered. "I know."

They were still, quiet, in perfect peace.

"Do I still have to leave?" he teased.

"Leave?" she asked.

"Don't you remember?"

"No, I don't," she said truthfully, for she couldn't remember anything in her state of hazy satisfaction.

"That's good," he said. "Let's forget everything and hold on to this moment in time."

"Yes," she agreed, not even sure what he meant. Time had no beginning or ending for her.

She shivered slightly and Nick pulled back the covers so they could crawl beneath them.

As Kara drifted to sleep, Nick held her tenderly, not wanting to break the physical contact. Their lovemaking had been so unexpected, so miraculous that he was afraid to let the moment pass. He smoothed back the strands of her hair that seemed always to be curling around her face. He felt affection and desire, mixed with a strange kind of confusion. He'd wanted her since the first time he'd seen her. That part was true. Now that they'd made love, everything would be different between them, but he wasn't sure just how.

In her sleep, Kara looked young and vulnerable, not at all like the wild-eyed harridan who'd charged into his apartment. She'd knocked him off his feet in more ways than one.

Nick grinned to himself, then shifted slightly so that Kara's head lay against his shoulder. He had no idea how Kara would react when morning came. But he rarely knew what would happen next with her. Whatever her response, it would be interesting. He'd have to take his cues from her.

When Kara woke up, Nick's leg was draped possessively over hers, his arm flung across her shoulder. She lay there, holding her breath and praying that he wouldn't open his eyes, praying that she could escape without having to face him in the bright morning light.

Finally, he stirred and turned over, and crablike she scurried to her side of the bed, dropped to the floor and gathered up her clothes. Embarrassment flooded through her as she touched each garment. Her bra, her panties, the shirt he'd pulled over her head, and the rumpled shorts. She flushed hotly at the memory of their making love. She could feel the warmth of his mouth on her breast and his hands caressing her. Kara's head swam as the images flooded her mind. What had possessed her to end up in bed with Nick Fleming?

Clutching her clothes, she tiptoed across the bedroom. She and Nick would have to talk over what had happened, but not now. She needed time alone to think about what the hell she was going to do.

Two hours later, after a shower, several cups of coffee and a change of clothes at the houseboat, Kara was on her way into Cypress Key. Mercifully, the boat had cooled off by early morning, so she'd had a chance to sit quietly, work out a simple diagnosis of her problem and come up with a solution. Nick brought out a latent aberration in her that she could only think of as insanity. He'd called her actions crazy when she arrived at his apartment, and he'd been right. But she realized that the craziness had begun not long after she'd met Nick. It had tempted her to stay in Cypress Key and run a restaurant against her better judgment. Then it had compelled her into his bed.

Insanity. That had to be it. Only a kind of madness would have driven her to the state of sensual abandon that she'd experienced last night. She felt a lurch in the pit of her stomach when she thought of all the intimate, erotic things they'd done in bed. But just because Nick was a wonderful lover didn't mean Kara should forget what had brought her to Florida. She had to get Nick *out* of her life so she could get *on* with her life.

Kara was the first client at the office of Hartwell Real Estate Company. She was lucky, the secretary informed her, that Mr. Hartwell had also arrived early and would have time to see her before his nine o'clock appointment. She could go right in.

"Good morning, Ms Selwyn. I'm Larry Hartwell. Can I get you some coffee? It's mighty early to be talking business."

"No coffee, thanks," Kara replied.

She sat down in the leather chair he indicated and glanced around the office. Plush and lush were the two words that came to her. The thick carpet, heavy draperies, polished mahogany desk, and original oil paintings suggested money and prestige.

"Well, now, what can I do for you today?" Larry Hartwell's appearance complemented his office perfectly in his tailor-made summer suit, pale blue shirt, conservative striped tie and highly polished shoes. He was young, in his early thirties, with blond hair combed back from a high forehead. He looked like just the kind of man her mother had always wanted her to date — smooth, polished, and probably very well connected.

Kara took a deep breath and plunged in. "I'm really not sure why I'm here, except that I've seen your ads in the newspaper and your billboards along the highway. I knew your company was large —"

"Biggest in the county," Larry said, with a glint of pride in his keen blue eyes.

"I was hoping you could give me some advice," she went on tentatively. Now that Kara was here, she was uncertain how to proceed.

"About the Sundowner?"

"How did you know that I was connected with the Sundowner?"

Just the hint of a grin curved Larry's lips. With one hand he smoothed back his perfectly trimmed blond hair and said, "Ms Selwyn, this is Cypress Key. Everybody knows everything. Or let me put it another way. Everybody who's anybody knows what's happening with the movers and shakers around here. I knew as soon as you hit town."

"I'm not exactly a mover or a shaker."

"The Sundowner's a popular spot, and you're making some waves over here. That qualifies you," he said with another grin. "So you and Fleming aren't seeing eye to eye about the place?"

"You know that, too?"

Larry nodded.

"Well, that saves me a lot of explaining. Nick — uh, Mr. Fleming and I own the Sundowner jointly. My father left it to both of us, and his lawyer says the will is legal."

Larry tapped his perfectly sharpened pencil against the desk blotter. "I thought that was pretty unusual, leaving the place to Fleming, too. Don't know where he came from, but he just kind of wormed his way into your daddy's business and ended up on top, didn't he?"

Kara assumed the question was rhetorical and didn't bother to answer.

"What do you know about Fleming's background?"

"Not much. He said he was born up north, in Pennsylvania, I think."

"Hmm. Well maybe we should look into that. He could have worked a scam of some kind on your daddy."

"Oh, no," Kara broke in. "That is, I don't think so. Nick — uh, Mr. Fleming might very well have a checkered past, but according to what everyone says, my father loved him like a son."

Larry lifted one eyebrow. "A good con artist can work a good scam."

"Well, maybe," Kara said thoughtfully.

"Wouldn't hurt to ask some questions around the Sundowner, kind of casually. You might come up with something that would help you get him out of the picture."

"That's what I want. Nick Fleming out of the picture so I can sell the restaurant. That's why I came down here to Cypress Key. To sell it," Kara said firmly. "I've just gotten sidetracked, and I don't like to be sidetracked."

"Well then," he said, leaning back in his chair and giving his hair another quick smoothing. "There're several things we need to do."

"I'll try anything," Kara told him.

"Okay. We can begin by digging up some dirt on Fleming. Check into his past." He hesitated and then added, "But I can tell by your face, you don't like that idea. Guess it could be uncomfortable, what with you and him working together."

And sleeping together, Kara thought. She hoped she wasn't blushing.

"What I *can* do is check the paper trail on the place, the title, the inspections, licenses. Might find something that'll give us a little leverage with Fleming."

"Like what?"

"I don't know for sure. Just let me nose around. You never can tell what might turn up."

Kara nodded. There couldn't be anything wrong with that.

"The other thing I'll do is see what kind of money package I can put together for the property, what kind of hungry investors are out there. I know Fleming doesn't want to sell, but if I went to him with a million-dollar deal, he just might decide he's ready to retire."

"Maybe," Kara said. "After all, we've been talking in abstractions, but if you really have a deal, he might listen."

"Money talks, Ms Selwyn."

"Kara, please."

"And I'm Larry. I'll get started on this right away, Kara," he said as she got up. "Meanwhile, I'd be happy to take you to lunch today or maybe dinner tonight."

Her response was quick. "Thanks so much, Larry, but I'll be working all day — lunch and dinner at the Sundowner. Whatever happens, I have to keep on with my plans to bring in new business."

"I understand that," Larry said. "Maybe another time." He followed her to the door.

Kara didn't respond directly but shook his hand instead. However, Larry didn't let it go at that. "I'll be in touch, Kara, and I look forward to seeing you again, both personally and professionally." He flashed an engaging smile.

"I'm sure we'll talk soon," Kara evaded, "but if I'm not at the Sundowner when you call, please don't leave a message. Nick doesn't need to know that we've talked."

"I'll speak to you or no one," Larry promised. "And I'm looking forward to seeing you real soon."

Kara walked quickly to her car, hoping Larry was as persistent a realtor as he was a suitor — but more successful. Obviously, he knew his business and was good at it. She should have talked to him two weeks ago before her life got so out of hand, Kara thought. Still, she found herself fighting feelings of guilt about continuing with her original plan to sell the Sundowner. There was no logical reason for the guilt. She had a right to explore every possibility that could lead to the eventual sale of the place. She was sure of that.

As Kara started her car and headed toward the restaurant, there was one more thing she was sure of: she wouldn't be dating Larry. No more entanglements with men in Cypress Key. There'd certainly be no more with Nick Fleming, she swore to herself. Anyone could make a mistake, and she wasn't going to let it happen again. What had occurred between them had shaken her deeply. She could no longer trust her own judgment, and her behavior was irrational, even dangerous.

Dangerous. That was the first impression that she'd had of Nick Fleming. And she'd been right.

8

Kara had no idea how she was going to handle running into Nick. So she put it off temporarily by slipping into the Sundowner without anyone seeing her.

She could hear Nick and Buck talking in the bar as she quickly sped by into the dining room. She looked around. Betty wasn't there, which was just as well. She didn't feel like talking to her, either. But there was work to be done so she headed for a table in the far corner, out of sight of the bar, and pulled out her notebook.

Even if Larry could find a way to make Nick sell, it might take weeks or months. Meanwhile, life would go on. She went over her plans. First, an ad for the local paper announcing the dining room's new luncheon hours, including a ten percent discount coupon for the first week's customers. Next, a classified ad to hire a waiter. That was a must. Kara knew from her experience with the Over Sixties Club that she wasn't server material.

As she began working on the ad copy, her mind started to wander and the notes turned to doodles. Nick was in the bar, not more than fifty feet away. She'd avoided meeting him or talking to him, but she couldn't avoid remembering him from last night.

Their lovemaking had been wonderful. That scared the hell out of her. It just couldn't be possible that she'd allowed herself to feel such a glow over Nick. Yet she felt it, so strongly that it made her ache. But she had to push that out of her mind. With great determination, Kara tried to return to the job at hand. The ads had to get done, and they had to get done today. She couldn't let images of Nick Fleming keep her from accomplishing her task.

Finally, she conquered the daydreams and got down to work. She'd almost finished when she felt a hand on her shoulder.

The touch startled her. She looked up to find Nick standing there.

"Don't sneak up on me like that," she accused.

"A little grouchy this morning, aren't we?" Nick pulled out a chair and sat down beside her. "*You* did some sneaking yourself earlier today. Sneaked right out of my room, Kara."

She could feel her face grow hot. "I didn't want to waken you," she said lamely.

"You were embarrassed, weren't you?" he said gently.

She met his eyes then. His look was serious, but she couldn't tell what was going on in his head. "Yes, I was embarrassed . . . and ashamed at my behavior."

"Ashamed?" He seemed truly surprised at

her words. "Ashamed," he repeated, "because we made love?"

"Shh," Kara warned. "Someone might hear you." She paused for a long moment and then explained, "I didn't come to your place for . . . for that. I didn't mean it to happen. I just got —"

"Carried away?" Nick asked softly.

"Yes, that and kind of . . . crazy. In fact you said yourself that I was acting like a crazy person."

An unreadable expression passed fleetingly over Nick's face and then was replaced immediately by a look as cold and hard as his words. "So," he said, "making love to me was the act of a crazy woman, something you never wanted to happen, something that you didn't really *feel*."

"Yes . . . that's it . . . sort of," she stammered.

He leaned toward her. "It wasn't that way for me, Kara. It was exciting and spontaneous, and I enjoyed every minute. I'm not sorry about it, but I guess you are."

"I wish I could explain, but I can't. I mean I can't put it into words."

"But you know how you feel?" The smile that curved his lips offered no amusement. "Ashamed and embarrassed. How complimentary." His words were as sharp as daggers. "You make everything so damned complicated, Kara."

Kara felt her eyes fill with tears. She didn't want to cry in front of him. "I'm sorry, Nick.

Sorry that it happened, sorry that we're fighting. But then we always seem to be fighting. That's been our true relationship."

"You could be right. Fighting is nothing unusual for us. Maybe the only place we can get along is in bed."

"But don't you understand?" she asked, swallowing her emotions. "It's impossible for us to be at loggerheads all day and then jump into bed and pretend nothing is the matter."

"Sounds like a good solution to me, but then it's your choice."

"Yes, it is," Kara agreed. "We have to come to terms with the problem and admit that this arrangement isn't working out. I never wanted to be at the Sundowner, and you didn't want me here. That hasn't changed."

"But I do want you here —"

"Only in bed, Nick," Kara reminded him. "You don't want me to be a part of the restaurant, you don't want me making improvements —"

"Let's call them changes," Nick said. "We aren't sure yet whether you've improved anything."

"Do you see what I mean about us?" Kara said, her anger growing. "We'll never agree about anything. That's why we should just give up working together, sell the place and divide the profits. That's the only way it'll ever work."

Nick stood up suddenly. "Do we have to go through all that again, Kara? I told you, the

Sundowner isn't for sale. And as for our relationship — or lack of it — I think you're right. Mixing business and pleasure causes problems. Betty and Arthur proved that when they were married."

"I certainly didn't mean for last night to happen. But it did, and all we can do now is try to forget it. Wipe the slate clean. Work out a way for us to get along in —"

"Peace and harmony. Sounds great," he commented sarcastically, "but not very practical. Do you have a plan?"

"Not really," Kara mumbled. "I hadn't thought about that part of it."

"Well, I suggest you start thinking, Kara." He grasped the edge of the table with both hands and leaned toward her. "Think about your terms, for instance."

"Terms?" Kara moved back away from him. She'd never seen Nick act so harsh.

"The terms of our working relationship. I assume you're going to keep on with your little experiment here in the dining room."

"Yes, I am, at least for now." Until Larry Hartwell came up with some answers for her, Kara thought.

"So?"

"So . . ." She searched frantically for a response and sighed with relief when the obvious one came to her. "Our paths simply don't need to cross. There's no reason for us to see each other except when we have to make joint decisions. As Betty said to Arthur, 'You go your way, and I'll go mine.' It's good advice that I think we can both handle."

"I can handle anything."

Kara was aware that he was studying her through narrowed eyes. A little shiver that started at the nape of her neck began to tingle down her spine. She felt as though she were a specimen under a microscope.

"After all," Nick went on, "I've handled everything you threw at me from the beginning."

"What are you talking about?"

"Let's face it, Kara. You turned every meeting between us into a conflict, and then when you realized what all those fireworks really meant, you backed away."

"The fireworks, as you call them, just meant we didn't like each other," she said.

"No, Kara, they meant exactly the opposite — you just don't want to admit it."

"What gives you the right to analyze my feelings like that?" Before he could respond, she went on, "You think you know everything about me, but you don't," she accused. "You know nothing, nothing!"

Nick ignored her outburst. "As I was saying, now that you know what the fireworks mean, you're more determined than ever to keep me at arm's length. Why can't you be honest about your feelings, Kara?"

Kara's throat constricted, and the tightness made answering difficult. She remembered

Larry's suspicions about Nick. And now Nick was questioning *her* honesty. She swallowed deeply. "I am being honest when I say that the best solution for us both is to remain professional, businesslike, and —"

"Distant," Nick finished. "Whatever you want, Kara. I'm willing to accept your version of last night. Let's just say it never happened." He reached in his pocket, pulled out a check and dropped it onto the table. "For you."

"What's this?" she asked.

"Don't be offended. It's not payment for services rendered. It's a check for a new air conditioner."

"I don't want it," Kara said stubbornly. "I'll buy my own."

"Take it," Nick growled. "As you mentioned last night, the houseboat is mine. I'm responsible for the repairs."

"I feel very awkward about this," she said.

"Well, don't let it worry you, Kara. You'll recover."

Not knowing what else to do, Kara responded to his sarcasm by picking up the check.

"Good," he said. "That makes everything easier because your accepting the check tells me you plan to stay on the houseboat and give up the idea of evicting me from Sean's place. *My* place," he corrected.

"Yes," she agreed. "It remains your place." The memory of everything she'd tried to forget about last night flooded over Kara. She knew her face was flushed. "I won't be paying you any more late-night visits," she finished.

"A loss for both of us," he said huskily.

Before she could react, their conversation was interrupted by a much louder encounter from the kitchen.

"Woman, where'd you put my shrimp knife? I bet you hid it from me," Arthur shouted.

"You stupid mule, it's right in the drawer where you left it. You're just too stubborn to admit you didn't see it," Betty countered.

"Can't see what's not there."

"Get outta my way. I'll find it."

Betty's words were followed by the sound of crashing cutlery.

Nick shrugged and headed for the bar. After a few steps he paused, looking back at Kara. "Works great, doesn't it?"

"What?" Kara asked.

"That philosophy of yours and Betty's — you go your way, and I'll go mine."

Kara didn't respond.

"Well, I leave Betty and Arthur to you, Kara. You hired her so you can take care of the problems she creates. I have enough of my own."

Kara got up and went to the kitchen, actually relieved to get her mind off her own problems.

"What's going on?" she asked as she pushed through the doors.

A drawer lay upside down beside a clutter of knives, spoons, stirrers and ladles. "Arthur was showing off his manly strength and pulled that drawer right out of the cabinet," Betty said.

Arthur glowered.

"Now he's got some cleaning to do."

"That woman," he said, pointing a finger at Betty, "has been messing in my stuff, and *she* can do the cleaning up."

"I —" Betty began.

"But not until she finds my shrimp knife."

"I never messed up your kitchen," Betty managed to say. "Kara and I spent two hours cleaning after the party yesterday, and I put everything back where it belonged."

"Then *where* is my shrimp knife?" Arthur demanded.

"Well, it was in the drawer, so I reckon it's on the floor now." Betty sauntered over to the pile of scattered implements and surveyed them carefully.

"Then you find it," Arthur demanded.

Betty leaned down gracefully and with a dramatic gesture that rattled the clunky bracelets on her arms, fished the knife from the pile and handed it to Arthur.

He took it without a word and carefully avoided Betty's dancing black eyes. An uncomfortable silence pervaded the kitchen.

Kara cleared her throat. "Um, well, this all worked out just fine, didn't it? Arthur has his shrimp knife, and Betty and I are off the hook." She smiled brightly.

Arthur crossed his arms across his chest.

Kara tried again. "The shrimp salad was

wonderful, Arthur. We appreciated it so much, didn't we, Betty?"

Betty nodded.

"I felt like making it," Arthur said. "Sometimes I do. And sometimes I don't."

"I know, I know, we all have days like that," Kara said placatingly. She had begun to inch her way back toward the door. Peace reigned, for the moment, and she was determined to take advantage of it to make her getaway.

Betty's next remark stopped her in midstep. "The shrimp salad at Ben Crowley's Grill is pretty good, too."

"Just how do you know that?" Arthur asked.

"Stopped by for take-out last night."

"I made shrimp salad at the Sundowner and you went to Crowley's?" Arthur asked threateningly.

"Yours was all gone."

"The women at the party just loved it, Arthur. Ate it all up in no time," Kara offered.

"So you decided to try Crowley's?"

"Yes, I did," Betty responded.

"Even though the man can't tell cilantro from basil?"

"Well, his use of herbs may not be subtle, but overall the food's not half-bad," Betty insisted. "And he *is* a charming gentleman. While I was waiting, he brought me a glass of wine. Said I looked tired. Said I looked like I needed a good massage."

143

"You let that man give you a massage?" Arthur roared.

"Did I say that?" Betty asked. "Kara, did I say that?"

Kara chose to stay out of the impending battle. "Ben Crowley is a perfect gentleman at all times. He said I *looked* like I needed a massage. Right here, where my muscles get so tense." Betty rubbed her neck, all the while watching Arthur's reaction.

"I know all about your muscles," he growled.

"Why, of course you do," Betty purred.

"And if you need a massage you just —"

"Just what, Arthur?" Betty asked.

"Just — just stay away from that Ben Crowley."

"Stay away?" Betty raised her voice in disbelief and headed toward Arthur, hands on her hips. "You're telling me what to do? I don't tell you what to do, and you have no business telling me —"

Arthur held his ground on the other side of the spilled utensils. "Some people just don't know what's best for them."

"Well, if you mean me, I know exactly what's best without listening to advice from you." She'd reached the utensil pile and it looked to Kara like nothing would stop her — not the utensils, not even Arthur.

Kara intervened, "I just remembered, Betty. We have a deadline to meet, and there's not a minute to lose." She reached out and grabbed Betty's arm.

"Wait," Arthur attempted.

"We have to get the classified ad ready for the newspaper," Kara continued as she maneuvered Betty a few feet away from the woman's adversary. "It's due at four o'clock, and if we don't get it in today, we won't make this week's edition." She pulled a little harder.

"Wait," Betty said, repeating Arthur's demand.

Kara wasn't about to listen to either one of them. "We're going. Now." While Arthur stood, glaring silently, she guided Betty out of the kitchen and into the dining room.

"What are you doing?" Kara asked Betty as they made their way across the room. "Trying to drive him crazy by taunting him about Crowley's?"

Betty smiled. Her earlier irritation had disappeared. "He sure is a jealous man, isn't he?"

"You're deliberately trying to make him jealous."

"I don't have to try. He was born that way."

"Betty, I know there's something going on between you and Arthur. You want him back, don't you? That's the reason you came to Cypress Key." She sat down at a table in the middle of the room, and Betty sat beside her, still smiling.

"Let's just say when it comes to me and my ex, it's the triumph of hope over experience.

Now what are we doing here? What's all this deadline business?"

Kara gave up her attempt to cope with the impossible situation between Betty and Arthur. "The classified ad. For a waiter."

"Oh, yes. A waiter." Betty chuckled a little wickedly. "Like we said before, someone young and cute. But I guess we can't put that in the paper."

"No, but I'm sure you'll be very selective in your interviewing." Kara showed Betty the ad.

"Looks good to me."

"Fine. We can get it into the next edition. Now we need to think about the best way to announce that we're open for lunch in the Ca-ribbean Room. Here's my idea." Kara shoved her notepad toward Betty. "Just a few words in bold type. No art at all. Inexpensive but catchy. I think that'll grab them, don't you?"

"Honey, you're an advertising genius," Betty said. "Now all we need is a discount coupon . . ."

"Here it is."

"When did you do all this?"

"Well, I've been thinking about it for a while, but I laid it all out today. I had a little extra time."

"My," Betty said. "It's just amazing. Why, I can take all this down to the paper, and they can run it just like it is. You even have the type sizes on here."

"Yes, I included all the specs. I don't think they'll have any problems."

"My, my," Betty said. "You sure are talented."

While Betty looked over the ad, Kara realized that it was the last thing on her mind. She was still thinking about the scene she'd just witnessed. Nick had said that fireworks between two people could mean more than conflict. According to Betty, the fireworks between her and Arthur meant passion. But what about Nick and Kara? Theirs was a volatile relationship, but the innate affection that she knew existed between Betty and Arthur was not there between her and Nick. Those two had the history of a loving relationship between them. Kara and Nick had been adversaries from the beginning.

And now, she thought, even the passion was gone. She knew that the true opposite of love was not hate but indifference. And that's what she'd seen on Nick's face when he'd stalked away from her this morning — cool indifference.

"Looks fine to me," Betty said. "You want me to drive this over to the paper?"

"That's a good idea, Betty. I don't think they'll have any problems with it, but if they do, just give me a call."

After Betty left, Kara realized she should have gone herself, should have taken the opportunity to get away from the Sundowner and Nick. Yet she hadn't; she'd chosen to stay right in the middle of what she could only think of as turmoil.

It didn't matter, though. Nick had gone off for a walk on the beach with Topaz. She'd watched them leave from the dining room. By the time she'd gone out on the deck and looked up the beach, they'd been out of sight. Now she had the place to herself, and she felt pretty sure that Nick had planned it that way. Although she was the one who'd suggested they go their separate ways, Nick was the one who'd taken her up on it.

Fine, Kara thought. Fine. She could handle the Caribbean Room perfectly well and, even though her mind occasionally wandered, she got the work done. Betty was right; the ads were very good, and she'd managed to turn them out in spite of her unsteady emotional state. Obviously, she wasn't as disturbed by Nick as she'd imagined.

Feeling more sure of herself, Kara headed for the bar where she knew she'd find Buck on duty. It was time to test the waters with him and the bar crowd, see what they were thinking about her plans. Not that it mattered. She'd continued with the Caribbean Room over Nick's objection; grumbles from the barflies certainly wouldn't stop her.

"Come on in, Kara, and have a drink. It's on the house." Buck chuckled at his own humor.

Kara took a seat at the bar and ordered her usual mineral water.

"I hear you've been mighty busy," he said, after he'd poured her a glass, added a twist of

148

lime and served it with a flourish.

"Oh?" Kara asked. Just what she'd expected; they'd been talking in the bar about yesterday's party.

"Yep. Heard you opened the place up and brought in a bunch of women."

Kara didn't like the way he said that, but she tried to ignore it. "I guess you also heard about Mrs. Perry's dress. I'm sure it's all over town by now that I missed her glass and poured iced tea down her bosom."

"Hard target to avoid," Buck said with a grin. "Don't quote me, but the old biddy could use some loosening up." He began polishing the bar with his spotless cloth.

"Otherwise, it was a nice event," Kara said with what pride she could muster.

"Planning to do it again next Monday?" Buck asked casually.

"Of course, if we get a request. Meanwhile, we'll be opening for lunch in there every day."

"Yeah, some of the men were talking about how there'd soon be women all over the place."

"And?" Kara prodded.

"Oh, nothing." Buck polished with renewed vigor.

"Come on, Buck. What did they say?" Kara asked warily.

"Just that all those women might . . . you know, cramp their style."

"Oh, did they?" Kara managed to avoid slamming her glass down on the bar. "And what might happen if their style got cramped?"

"Well, they might just stay away at lunch-time." Buck glanced sideways at Kara, waiting for her reaction.

It surprised *her*, so she imagined it probably surprised Buck as well. "That's fine! If they stay away, then we women can just take over the whole place, the dining room and bar, too. We'll have fashion shows and cosmetics demonstrations, kitchenware parties, maybe even bridal showers." Sarcasm dripped from her words. "Why, there's no end to the events we could have here at lunchtime if there were no men around."

"I didn't mean to rile you, Kara. I was just warning you about how the men were feeling."

"Who said I was riled?" Kara knew she couldn't put up the front much longer because the tears were beginning to form in her eyes.

Just before they spilled over, one of the stragglers from lunch ordered another beer, and Buck went off to serve him. Kara took a deep breath. Nick didn't want her around. Now it seemed Buck and his cronies felt the same way. Led by Mrs. Perry, the women would probably sign a petition to run her out of town!

Kara took another swig of her drink and tried not to think about the past twenty-four hours which were among the worst in her life. And her day showed no signs of improving.

She didn't even notice when Melissa slid onto a stool beside her.

"What's the matter, Kara?" she asked. "You look a little depressed."

"Who, me?" Kara managed a smile.

"Yes," Melissa insisted. "I have a feeling things aren't going so well, and I don't want to add to your problems, but —"

"Oh, go ahead, Melissa. Add to them," Kara insisted.

"Well, some of the waitresses have been asking me to talk to you."

Kara hadn't the slightest idea what was coming next, but something told her it wasn't going to be good news.

"I really don't like saying this. . . ."

"No one likes saying things today, but everyone seems to get around to them just the same," Kara commented. "Go on, Melissa."

"We heard you were going to hire waiters for the lunch crowd, and some of us . . . some of the waitresses . . . felt that would be unfair."

"But it wasn't unfair to the men when Nick filled the place up with beautiful women?"

"I guess that's beside the point now," Melissa said. "We're here, and no one ever complained. But you know that it's not legal to specify sex in ads, Kara."

"For major corporations, maybe, but not for the Sundowner," Kara argued.

"For any business with more than fifteen employees. And we're getting close to that number. I'm taking a course in business law, and I really try to keep up with things."

Kara began to feel utterly defeated. "So Nick can hire women to wear those ridiculous costumes with no problem, but I can't hire one man to wait on customers in the dining room?" Kara raised her eyes to the ceiling. "Is there no justice in the world?"

"It's not a big deal, Kara, but I thought you should know."

"Oh, it's a big deal, Melissa, just like everything else around here. I imagine if I hire a man, someone will sue me."

"I didn't say that. I don't think anyone would actually sue, but they'd be unhappy. One of the waitresses talked about picketing and another said she'd write a letter to the newspaper —"

"I can't believe this," Kara said. "Everything I do backfires."

"I know you work hard, but there are certain realities in running a restaurant."

"And I'm getting a crash course in reality today." Kara slid off the stool. She was thinking about a way to rally herself against the latest disaster, and it came to her before her feet touched the floor.

"In this day and age, I think you'll agree that 'waiter' can apply to a person of either sex. We're advertising for a waiter in the next issue of the newspaper. I'll interview everyone who applies, including any of the women who would like to change shifts. Then *I'll* reach a decision," Kara added.

"Oh, I'm sure you will, Kara. I'd hate for you

to get discouraged and leave."

"Discouraged?" Kara laughed unhappily. "That's hardly the word. But don't worry about my leaving. I'm staying put, Melissa." As she turned away, she called over her shoulder, "And if anyone asks, I'm on the way to town to buy an air conditioner. Then I'm going home to enjoy it."

Kara left the bar and headed for the deck. It had been her promise to take time out every night and watch the sun go down. She forced herself to do so, but the glowing hues held no magic for her tonight. They only served to re-mind her of what had happened in the short time since the last sunset.

Kara went down the stairs, across the parking lot and to her car. She'd done only one smart thing between those two sunsets: she'd met with Larry Hartwell. Somehow, that balanced the scales.

9

"Business is really picking up, eh, Nick?" Buck asked. Nick looked around the bar and then back at Buck.

"Looks about the same to me."

"The same as when?"

"As usual, Buck," Nick commented.

"Maybe. But not the same as a couple of weeks ago when Kara opened the dining room to all those hen parties."

"Hmm."

"You know what I'm talking about. When she started serving her lunches, you could shoot off a cannon in this place and not hit a living soul. Some of the guys started boycotting us. You thought they'd be gone for good, didn't you?" Before Nick could respond, Buck added, "So did I, to tell you the truth. Had a few uneasy days there. Then the regulars started drifting back. Now we're doing business as usual, maybe even a little better. Guess the guys realized those women weren't gonna take over their domain after all."

Nick leaned against the bar and looked across at Buck. "Okay, Buck, what are you getting at?"

"Nothing." Buck picked up a wineglass and

began rubbing it with a cloth. "Just making conversation."

"About *her*."

"You can't keep ignoring her, Nick."

"I've been doing a pretty good job of it so far." Nick had managed to avoid Kara by telling himself that she was the kind of woman who was dangerous for his mental health. The kind who made life damned complex, who couldn't enjoy a night of great lovemaking without turning it into a drama the next day. Women were difficult, especially that one.

"The farther I stay away from her, the better," he told Buck. "She runs the restaurant, I run the bar."

"Maybe. Doesn't keep you from watching her, though," Buck replied.

Nick poured himself a cup of coffee. "You're beginning to irritate me, Buck," he said. "I don't want to talk about her."

"Maybe," Buck repeated. "Doesn't keep you from thinking about her, though."

"How the devil do you know what I'm thinking about?"

"It shows," Buck observed. "She probably notices, too. 'Course, I expect you can tell she's also thinking about you. 'Cause she is."

"The wise old philosopher and mind reader. That's the problem with bartenders, they always have to spout their opinions to everyone in sight."

"Is that right? I thought bartenders had a

reputation for being good listeners."

"You're the exception to the rule."

"Oh, I listen good, Nick. Whenever somebody talks. You don't do much talking recently. So I have to do it for you. Except I don't have to tell you how well Kara's doing with her lunch crowd. There's a women's club in there today. Gonna be regulars, I hear. Then there's a sweet-sixteen birthday party coming up —"

Nick groaned. "Sean would turn over in his grave if he heard that."

"Maybe, but he wouldn't mind the business the Caribbean Room's bringing in."

"He'd think the name was ridiculous."

"What about the way Kara and Betty are turning themselves out in those bright-colored skirts? He'd go for that. I can go for their off-the-shoulder blouses myself. And the customers eat it up. It's atmosphere, Nick."

Nick drank his coffee in silence.

"So's the waiter," Buck said.

"He's atmosphere?"

"Sure. The lunch crowd loves him, and so do the waitresses. Never thought that would happen, did you?"

"Frankly, no. I was expecting a revolution."

"Naw, they love him. Besides, since he only works during the week, two of the waitresses get to take his weekend shifts, so everybody's happy."

"Well, he seems to be a nice guy, and at least he's married. Last thing I need around here is more people emotionally involved with each other."

Buck stopped his polishing and looked across at Nick. "Who're you talking about now, you and Kara?"

"I'm talking about Betty and Arthur, and you know it," Nick said. He certainly wasn't involved with Kara. They'd had a one-night stand which didn't mean much in the whole scheme of his life. The irritating part was that he couldn't get her off his mind. He was thinking about her all the time. Buck was right about that. He was thinking what it was like to hold her and kiss her . . .

"Sure," Buck said.

"What?" Nick had been lost in his reverie.

"Sure you're talking about Betty and Arthur. I knew that all along," Buck said with a twinkle in his eye.

"This coffee's stale, Buck. Better fix another pot," Nick said.

"Sure thing. Oh, here comes your 'atmosphere'," he added as Michael strode across the room. "Have a beer, Mike."

"No, thanks. Just taking a cigarette break."

"Lunch rush finished?" Buck asked.

"Yep. The last table's just paying the bill so the boss told me to take a few minutes off."

"The boss," Nick muttered under his breath.

"Looked like a pretty full house today," Buck commented conversationally.

"Yeah, we had a good day. Lots of compliments on the food."

Nick remained silent while the two men talked.

"Betty make something special?" Buck asked.

"Not Betty," Michael said. "Arthur. He came up with a new dish. Calls it Jamaican Grouper Arturo. The customers are crazy over it. He grills the fish and then adds a real spicy tomato sauce."

"Arthur's cooking for the lunch crowd?" Buck had a look of astonishment on his face.

"About once or twice a week he turns out a surprise for us. We make it the special of the day. The customers really go for it."

Nick finally came back into the conversation with a comment that echoed Buck's surprise. "Arthur cooking for Kara . . . how did she talk him into it?"

Michael put his cigarette out in the ashtray. "I don't think he's doing it for Kara. I think it's Betty. She and Arthur, well, they're getting pretty involved, it seems to me. They've been driving to work together, just for starters. And there's lots more. Something's going on."

Nick groaned. More damned complications. Something was going on between Betty and Arthur again. The signs were there no matter how hard he'd tried to ignore them. But lately he'd become an expert at ignoring emotions, especially his own.

The last of the lunch crowd was leaving the restaurant when Betty sang out in a musical voice, "Come on in here, Michael."

"That's my call to action." Michael headed for the dining room.

"You, too, Buck." Betty's voice had a sense of urgency to it.

"What in the world?" Buck looked at Nick, who shrugged.

"And Nick, are you there?" Betty called.

"I'm here."

"Then come on, all of you. Something's happening in here."

A feeling of foreboding went through Nick as he followed Buck toward the dining room.

They were all there. Michael, Kara, the two daytime kitchen helpers, and a waitress from the bar, all gathered around Betty and Arthur.

"Whaddya think this is, some kind of general strike?" Buck asked Nick as they approached the group.

"Your guess is as good as mine, but I'm prepared for the worst."

"I'd be inclined to agree with you except for one thing."

"What's that, Buck?"

"Betty and Arthur. Look at them. If they don't look like two lovebirds, I miss my guess."

Buck was right. The couple was standing very close together, and as he and Buck joined the circle, Nick saw that they were holding hands. His eyes met Arthur's in disbelief. Arthur nodded and then, to Nick's amazement, blushed.

"We're all here. So you can tell them now, darlin'," Betty urged. She gave Arthur's hand a little squeeze and pushed him forward.

Arthur cleared his throat dramatically. "Well, folks, I just want to say that I'm . . ."

Betty didn't let him pause very long. "Go on, honey."

"What I mean is, I'm proud to tell you Betty has done me the honor of . . ."

All eyes were on Arthur. Even Topaz, who'd come to see what was going on, sat at Arthur's feet and seemed to be nudging Arthur from the other side.

"She's agreed to be my wife," Arthur blurted out finally. "Again."

Kara led the applause, and Buck let out a mighty cheer. Only Nick was quiet, still stunned in disbelief.

"And since I just love being a June bride," Betty said with a laugh, "we're going to repeat our first June wedding — next week. Right here at the Sundowner if that's agreeable with everybody."

She was looking at Nick, but Kara answered. "Agreeable? It's fantastic. The Sundowner's a perfect place for a wedding. We can have it in this room. Or maybe out on the deck."

"The deck would be wonderful," Betty chimed. "I love outdoor weddings."

"Perfect. We'll fix it with flowers, bring in a band, champagne, the works."

Arthur turned to Nick. "Is it all right with you?" he asked.

"Of course. We're all family." He clapped Arthur on the back and gave Betty a hug. "We'll close the Sundowner, invite all your friends, and make this the best party of the year."

Cheers went up in the room as everyone crowded around Arthur and Betty. All except Nick, who stood to one side. When Kara glanced over at him, she noticed he wasn't looking at the happy couple. He was looking at her. Deliberately she turned her head and looked away.

Nick cursed and tugged at his bow tie. "I know it's your wedding day, Arthur. But couldn't you have done without these monkey suits?"

"It was Betty's idea. She wanted a formal wedding with us in dinner jackets. I don't like it any better than you."

"We could have just worn dark suits."

"Nick, you don't have a dark suit, and neither do I." Arthur laughed. "Better to rent the formal stuff than to go out and buy a suit."

"That's true," Nick admitted. "But with a suit I could have worn a regular tie. I'll never get this thing right." He stepped in front of the mirror, tried again and failed. "Couldn't you two have gotten married at city hall?"

"That's what we did the first time. I guess Betty thinks if we make a big deal of it today, it'll last."

"And what do you think, Arthur? We've been

friends a long time. Give me the real story."

"Here, let me fix that for you. You'll be all day." Arthur loosened Nick's bow tie and created a perfect knot. "There." He stepped back and admired his handiwork. "What do I think?"

"That's what I asked you, old buddy."

"It's hard to explain."

"Try."

"Well, a woman like Betty gets in your blood. You can't live with her, and you sure can't live without her. She makes me crazy."

"Not much of a recommendation."

"Sure it is, Nick. It's the kind of craziness I need. I'm wild over her. I just love that woman to death."

"Maybe the two of you should have tried living together for a while."

"Not a chance. For Betty, it's marriage or nothing. And to tell you the truth, it's the same for me." Arthur handed Nick a white carnation.

"What's this for?"

"For my best man. Put it in your lapel."

"Oh. All right." Nick tried threading the stem of the flower through the fake buttonhole in his lapel, without much success.

"It's a good thing this is my last wedding. Getting you ready is a real chore," Arthur said. "It's called a boutonniere, and it goes like this." He pinned it to Nick's lapel. "You still look worried, what is it?"

"Nothing."

"You think there're gonna be problems in the kitchen between Betty and me? Forget it. She'll do lunch, and I'll do dinner. There won't be any disagreements this time."

"I hope you're right. Things have been stirred up enough around here since . . . well, for the past month or two. But that's not really what's bothering me."

"Oh?"

"No, I'm worried about something much more serious."

"What's that, Nick?"

"During the ceremony, when it comes time for me to give you the ring, what if I drop it?"

Arthur let out a melodious laugh. "You wouldn't dare."

The sound of piano music surged up from below. "Now, let's get downstairs. I'm ready to get myself married."

Kara heard the music with a shiver of anticipation. Her fingers trembling, she straightened the coronet of silk flowers on Betty's dark hair for the tenth time.

"It looks fine, Kara. Don't keep fretting over it."

"I can't help it. I'm so nervous." Kara managed a laugh. "*I'm* nervous, and you're getting married!"

"I'm calm as a clam."

"It's not possible," Kara objected.

"Sure it is, honey, 'cause I know what I'm

doing this time. I'm marrying the man I love, and I couldn't be more sure of myself. Never should have divorced Arthur in the first place. I missed him from the very first day I left him, and I never stopped. It's just that way with some men and women — they're born to be together." With noticeably steady hands, Betty touched the coronet and nodded to Kara in satisfaction. Then she smiled slyly. "It's just like that with you and Nick."

"What? Don't be ridiculous, Betty. Nick and I shouldn't even be mentioned in the same sentence. Now, turn around, and let me see the back."

"My back is just fine, so don't you change the subject," Betty chided. "I see him watching you. I see you watching him."

"No, you don't."

"Yes, I do." Betty grinned.

"Nick and I are business partners. No, not even partners. We're associates, and if I *am* watching him, it's to see he doesn't rob me blind. He goes his way, I go mine."

Betty's grin turned into a full resonant laugh. "Yes, I know. Just like me and Arthur."

From downstairs, they heard the pianist begin to triumphantly thump out the wedding march. "Come on, maid of honor. They're playing my song!"

The sun shone brightly and a faint breeze barely ruffled Kara's hair as she stepped forward to the music. She moved solemnly along the red carpet that had been placed over the deck, and the guests turned to watch her approach. In the distance, the waves at low tide lapped gently on the shore.

Arthur looked very serious standing beside the minister. A little smile flickered over his lips, and Kara thought she saw a nod of approval as she made it to the end of the deck and took her place beside Nick. She'd managed throughout the long walk to keep time with the music — and to avoid looking at Nick. Until now.

She had to acknowledge him. She did so with a smile, which he returned a little wryly, she thought. Betty had said he watched her all the time, and he was certainly watching her now. The intensity of his gaze made her uncomfortable, but she couldn't take her eyes from his. She tried to smile again. Her lips were dry, and she could feel them tremble. What Betty said was nonsense. They were *not* born to be together. All that togetherness was for Arthur and Betty. Not for her and Nick. Never.

Nick took in everything at once. The cobalt blue of her dress, the silky softness as it billowed around her. The flowers tucked in her hair. She looked so damned good it made him ache. She was fresh and young and vibrant. When he was near her he could almost feel the energy that emanated from her. It drew him like a magnet. It was drawing him now. He couldn't stop looking at her.

Nick finally pulled his gaze from Kara as the music changed tempo and Betty appeared. They all turned to watch her come out of the Sundowner on Buck's arm, regal and sophisticated in her pale pink lace dress. Buck didn't even try to hide his excitement. He looked like a proud father.

The minister stepped forward. Betty smiled dazzlingly at Arthur, and the ceremony began.

Hours later, Nick pulled off his dinner jacket, loosened his tie and leaned back against the kitchen counter, a glass of champagne in his hand.

"So what in the world did you do to my dog?"

Topaz sat at his feet, pink tongue lolling out of his mouth. Around the dog's neck was a colorful bouquet of flowers.

Kara carefully wrapped the last of the wedding cake in foil. All the other leftovers had been put away, the dishes stacked for tomorrow's cleaning crew, and the last of the guests had left. "You mean his collar? I thought it was rather festive." Kara continued with her chore.

"He looks like a sissy. How'd you do it?" he asked.

Kara put the cake in the refrigerator. "Artificial flowers and a little glue. Pretty cute, eh?"

"Topaz is a macho dog — he's *never* cute."

Kara noticed the teasing look on Nick's face

and relaxed a little. This was the first time they'd been alone in three weeks. She was still riding high on euphoria from the wedding celebration, and she could tell that Nick was in a good mood, too, probably because he'd finally shed his jacket and undone his bow tie. In a way, that was too bad because he'd looked very handsome in his formal clothes, especially to Kara, who'd rarely even seen him in long pants. A shorts-and-T-shirt type, he cut quite a figure in dinner jacket, black trousers, bow tie and boutonniere.

Maybe, just maybe, they could avoid a fight this time.

"Have some champagne with me," he offered. "There's nothing more to do here."

"Well —"

"Come on, Kara. There's no reason for you to go back to the boat except to watch the river flow. And," he added as he led Kara into the bar, "we need to toast the newlyweds."

"We already did." Kara followed along anyway, without protesting further.

"This is a special toast, a more personal one."

"Which they aren't even here to appreciate."

"That's all right." Nick poured Kara a glass of champagne from an open bottle. "They know we're thinking about them."

Nick raised his glass and Kara clinked hers against it.

"Here's to Betty and Arthur," Nick said.

"And to true love —"

"The second time around."

Nick downed the champagne, but Kara leaned back against the bar and sipped hers slowly. "This is the first moment I've had to relax since the ceremony."

"You were very busy," he noted. "Too busy to dance."

"I danced once with Arthur. No, twice," she corrected. "And I danced with Buck."

"But not with me."

"You didn't ask me." Kara echoed his light, teasing tone. Both of them were too tired to have their defenses up, she decided. Maybe they were still caught up in the glow of happiness that had radiated from the newlyweds. After all, weddings were a time for joy. Any other mood would have been inappropriate to the occasion.

"No, I didn't ask you," Nick agreed. "But I thought about it."

Kara laughed. "I couldn't read your mind."

"I wasn't sure you'd want to dance, or even get close to me. Besides, I was afraid if I approached you, I might put you in a bad mood. And I knew how dangerous that can be."

Kara remembered, a little regretfully. "I don't throw vases in public, especially at weddings."

"I had a feeling that was the case, but I didn't want to take any chances. Now, however, since there's no one around . . ." Nick walked over to the jukebox, fished for a quarter and dropped it in. Then he turned to her, his hand extended. "Come on. One dance. For Betty and Arthur. For the spirit of love and forgiveness."

"Well —"

"Think about it, Kara. If those two can get married, then we certainly should be able to manage a dance together. Come on, there's not a single vase in the bar."

"And I wouldn't throw it if there were," Kara replied. One dance couldn't hurt; in fact, it could go a long way toward wiping out the bitterness. He'd already taken a step in that direction with his jovial mood. This dance would take them the rest of the way.

She stepped toward him and reached for his hand. "Let's take advantage of the good wedding karma."

The music he'd selected was soft and romantic, a mellow saxophone leading strings and woodwinds in a sensual melody. But the moment Kara's hand touched him, she realized she'd made a mistake.

The warmth of his touch spread through her and signaled immediate danger. She sensed an awareness in his eyes, and in his voice as he spoke her name and pulled her closer. They stood facing each other, and Nick put his free hand on the small of her back as he began to move with the music.

Her breasts made contact with his chest, her

hips skimmed his, and they were dancing, but too close, much too close. Kara abruptly moved back a step.

"Oh, I forgot, arm's length."

Kara took a deep breath and tried to relax. "Sorry."

"Is this what they taught you at dancing school back in Atlanta, Miss Selwyn?"

"The teacher *did* insist on a discreet space between partners. And yes, it was at my dancing school back in Atlanta," Kara admitted.

"I knew it."

They danced on, still separated slightly.

"But you're all grown up now, Kara. And you're dancing with me, not your twelve-year-old partner."

Kara smiled and stepped closer to him. Then, just as she'd learned at dancing class, she attempted to make polite conversation. "And where did you learn? At school?"

"Nope. I never went to a school dance."

"Not even a class prom?" Kara asked in surprise.

"I dropped out of school pretty early, wasn't much of a scholar." Nick was quiet for a while before adding, "Life was pretty tough where I grew up. I had to work, help out at home. There wasn't a lot of time for proms."

Kara could feel his breath fluttering her hair, and when she lay her head against his shoulder, she could hear the steady beating of his heart. "You missed out on so much that kids take for granted," she said.

"Some of them, maybe. I was on my own at an early age." The low rumble of his voice reverberated in his chest.

Kara let herself move with him, and a delicious warmth began to drift over her like the night breeze. He tightened his arm around her and pulled her closer. They could have been the only two people in the world. It was a beautiful moment, and Kara gave herself to it.

Nick looked at her through half-closed eyes. "We're doing okay, aren't we?" He sounded a little surprised.

"We can get along if we try — even though you never took dancing lessons," Kara teased lightly. "Besides, you dance wonderfully."

"More than dancing school separates us, Kara. We come from entirely different backgrounds, different worlds."

"That's not why we argue. It has nothing to do with how we were brought up. We just got off on the wrong foot right from the beginning."

"I'll say," he agreed.

"It's not good for business," she said.

"Or pleasure."

"Now it's time to apologize and start all over." Kara's expression was very serious, determined.

Nick stopped dancing and stood still. He ran

his fingers through her hair in a distracted, gentle way. "I'd like that to happen. I'd like to kiss and make up."

"I didn't mean —"

"But you did," he told her.

She knew he was right, and just that knowledge sent a shiver vibrating up Kara's spine. She looked up at him. His face was very close, and he seemed young and vulnerable. She *did* want to kiss him, to close the gap between them.

Nick wrapped both arms around her. The music had ended, and silence pervaded the bar. The doors were closed, and not even the whisper of the surf invaded their privacy. There was only one sound, the dual beating, wild and erratic, of their hearts.

She raised her hand and touched his cheek, preparing to tell him that she wanted his kiss, his mouth on hers. "Nick —"

She didn't have to say the words. Nick knew. His heart convulsed inside his chest at the touch of her hand, the scent of her perfume, the nearness of her. Holding her so close set him on fire.

Maybe he'd been a fool to ask her to dance. Maybe it was madness to hold her. But it was a madness he couldn't escape. Her lips were only inches away. He had to kiss her.

She touched her top lip nervously with the tip of her tongue, and the innocent action drove him over the edge.

"Kara —"

Nick brought his mouth down on hers in a kiss of dizzying hunger. She softened in his arms, opened like a flower beneath his kiss. He felt the warmth of her curves against him, her soft breasts, rounded hips, firm thighs. He moved his hands along her body, cupped her bottom and pulled her even closer.

Their kiss grew more frenzied until Kara felt that she would go mad with desire. A vision flashed through her mind of her and Nick in bed, their bodies damp with lovemaking. The image teased her with its promise of pleasure. The only way to fulfill her need would be for the vision to become reality.

Nick tore his mouth away from hers. She could feel his heart pounding and his breath coming in quick, rough gasps. "Tell me now, Kara, if you want me to stop. If you don't tell me now, I won't be able to —"

"Then don't," she cried. "Don't stop." She pressed closer to him.

"I want you so much. I'm not sure I can wait 'tll we get upstairs."

"You don't have to," Kara said. "Look behind us." By the bar was a colorful wall hanging. In one quick movement, Nick pulled it down, spread it on the floor and lowered Kara onto the soft, woven cotton.

Nick smiled appreciatively. "You have a wonderful sense of adventure. I —"

Kara cut off his words with her kiss. She met his lips boldly, kissing him as he had kissed her.

She felt the stubble on his cheek, rough against her face and tasted the moist sweetness of his tongue.

Their hands roamed over each other's bodies, pulling at buttons and zippers until their clothes were shed and lay tangled on the floor.

Kara's warm flesh grew feverish as Nick's hands explored her naked body. She felt hot breath at her neck, her breasts, along the line of her hips. His tongue ignited a burning need between her legs.

Hardly able to control herself, Kara flung back her head and called out Nick's name. His touch inflamed her whole body. Together they created an unbearable heat from which there was no relief.

"Nick —"

"I know," he said. "I know." He lifted his head and looked at her across the length of her body. "I want to be inside of you," he said.

"Yes," she cried.

He raised himself until he was kneeling over her. Then he touched her between the legs and parted her soft femininity, preparing her for his entry. When it happened Kara gasped with pleasure. As her body encompassed his erection, it grew stronger inside her. Hot and moist, they moved together.

Kara held back nothing. From the back of her throat little moans escaped each time he filled her, withdrew and filled her again. The moans turned to cries of ecstasy. She felt him deep inside, held him fast, and then let him go, sure that nothing could equal that instant of passion. Then it happened again — and again.

Nick looked down at Kara. The heat of her passion seemed to have taken over her whole body. Her wide blue eyes were fiery with pleasure, her copper-colored hair was bright as a flame. The rapture on her face reflected what he felt. Then he plunged into her once again, fired by her response.

She reacted to him as never before, arching her back and holding him so tightly that her fingers gouged into his back. She gave herself to the spasm of pleasure that shot through her, then exploded in a thousand fiery fragments.

"Oh, Nick," she whispered. She lay trembling in his arms, clinging to him.

He held her damp body tightly against his. He was still shaking from the power of their lovemaking even as he tried to calm her tremors.

Finally they both began to breathe more evenly, and he clambered to his knees and scooped her up.

"Where're we going?"

"Upstairs," he whispered. "To my bed. Our bed. I want to make love to you all night, Kara. I want to make love to you until we can't move or talk or even think."

He was halfway across the room when he stopped. "Unless you're too . . . ashamed." He repeated what he'd said to her after the first time, the only other time, they'd made love. His face was serious and questioning.

Kara looked back at him. tears shimmering in her eyes. "I was never ashamed, Nick," she said. "I . . . I was scared."

"Scared?" He kissed her forehead tenderly. "Why, Kara?"

"Because, you idiot, I'm in love with you."

At first she thought he was going to drop her, but he held on. A look of wonder transfigured his face. "In love? You . . ."

Kara looked at him evenly, her tears gone. "No more talk, Nick Fleming."

"But —"

"Now's the time for action."

Nick laughed aloud. "Action it is." He headed toward the stairs to his apartment, Kara in his arms. "Never let it be said that I didn't oblige my partner."

10

Nick stood by his bedroom window, wearing only an old pair of shorts. He turned from the view and looked across the room at Kara, snuggled up on his bed, just awakening.

"You didn't run away." Nick couldn't keep the relief out of his voice.

Kara sat up and wrapped the sheet around her torso. The sunlight that streamed through the window cut a bright pattern across the floor and highlighted Kara's tousled red hair.

"I was too . . ." She struggled for the right word. "Too . . . satisfied to move." She tugged at the sheet to make sure it completely covered her breasts.

"You don't have to cover up," he said gently.

"I get shy in the light of day, I guess. Besides, you're up and dressed —"

"If you call this dressed. Same shorts. Same lack of shirt and shoes."

"That's about as dressed as I've ever seen you, except for yesterday in your tux, of course.

"When I felt very idiotic."

"And looked very handsome."

"Anyway, you're at least partially dressed and I'm still lying around, naked and lazy." Kara fluffed the pillows behind her and burrowed into them happily.

"Just the way I like you." Nick sat down on the corner of the bed. Once more he noticed her hand tugging at the sheet. "Kara, you can't be shy with me now." He leaned over and kissed her bare shoulder above the sheet. "Not after last night."

She blushed slightly but didn't avert her eyes as she reached up to touch his face. It was a gesture Nick loved so much, gentle and tender.

He put his hand over hers, and the look she gave him was loving. *She* was loving. She'd even said that she loved him last night. Kara was a beautiful, passionate woman, but she gave her love too freely. She knew nothing about him, and there was a lot to know.

Nick turned her hand over and kissed the palm. Then he remembered. "I brought breakfast." On the bedside table was a tray. "Coffee. And wedding cake."

Kara laughed. "Of course. Why not have wedding cake for breakfast?"

"I put sugar and a little milk in your coffee." He handed her the cup. "That was a guess. You probably like it black."

"Not at all. 'Sugar and a little milk' is exactly the way I like it. You must have read my mind. It's perfect, and so is the wedding cake." She opened her mouth as he brought a forkful of it to her lips. "You should be around everyday to serve breakfast in bed."

"Sounds like a good idea to me." Nick sat and watched Kara drink her coffee and nibble at the cake. "Aren't you having anything?" she asked between bites.

"I already had coffee, and the idea of cake for breakfast doesn't appeal to me at all."

"But you knew I'd like it?"

He leaned back beside her on the bed. "I guess I did."

"You seem to know a lot about me." Kara sipped her coffee.

"Sean told me a great deal, all he knew. That didn't include eating cake for breakfast, but I feel like I know you. Certainly better than you know me." He looked at her silently for a long moment.

Kara saw something on his face that she didn't understand. "What's wrong, Nick?"

"We need to talk." His jaw clenched and his face seemed to harden. Abruptly he got up and moved to a chair at the foot of the bed.

Kara put her coffee cup on the table. The look on her face registered alarm. "Last night . . . was something wrong?"

Nick shook his head vehemently. "No, Kara, there was nothing wrong. Everything was very right. That's the problem."

Kara felt a terrible sinking sensation in her stomach. He'd spoken no words of love to her this morning or even the night before when they'd been so consumed by each other. But she'd told him that she loved him. Now she was afraid that might have put him off. Her heart beat jerkily. "Now I *am* scared, Nick. Please tell

179

me what you're thinking."

"I'm thinking . . ." He hesitated and then the words rushed out. "I'm thinking that you don't know anything about me, Kara. I'm not the kind of guy you should fall in love with."

"I don't care about your past, Nick. That doesn't matter."

"My past is part of me, as yours is part of you, Kara. The past impacts on the present, and some of my rough edges are still visible. I don't like you to see them."

"Oh, Nick." Kara's words reflected a sense of relief. "I can handle your past." Whatever had happened to him before they met had nothing to do with him now. Nothing to do with *them*. "Please come over here by me so I can touch you, hold your hand."

Nick shook his head. "I want to tell you from here." Kara watched him as he shifted in the chair. His dark hair, still damp from the shower, fell across his forehead. His bronzed skin seemed to gleam in the morning sunlight. To Kara, Nick was a special man. She loved him, no matter what he was about to tell her.

"My dad ran off when I was three." Nick leaned back in the chair with his eyes closed. "My mom was pretty bitter, and I guess she took it out on me sometimes. She was sick a lot with respiratory problems, and when I was thirteen she died of pneumonia. Things had been pretty bad up until then. They got worse. No one in the family wanted me because I was such a hell-raiser. So I ran away. I started working in gyms, cleaning up, and later sparring with some of the lightweights. I could usually find a bed in the back room. I started fighting professionally when I was seventeen."

"You were a boxer? I thought your nose had been broken but I didn't realize . . ."

Nick opened his eyes and looked at Kara. "Happened in the ring. I was lucky to get away with only a broken nose since I really wasn't that great a fighter. I ended up in Miami fighting preliminary bouts on second-rate bills. An aging has-been, who could be paid off to take a fall. It's not a very glorious past, Kara."

"I'm sure you did your best," Kara attempted.

"No, I don't think I did. I probably didn't know what my best was. I finally drifted up the west coast to Florida and one night wandered into the Sundowner. I started talking to your dad over a beer. Out of the blue he offered me a job as a combination bartender and occasional bouncer. This place was rougher back then. Anyway, I took the job. I guess Sean recognized a sundowner like himself."

"Sundowner?" Kara was puzzled. "What do you mean?"

"It's a slang word Sean used to refer to himself. That's how this place got its name. It's a hobo, a tramp. A guy who arrives at sundown looking for a handout. Sean saw that in me, but luckily he saw more."

Leaning forward as she listened intently to Nick's words, Kara ignored the sheet that had slipped away from her shoulders.

"Sean was everything to me, Kara. I learned so much from him. He taught me to read." Nick saw the look on Kara's face and responded quickly. "Sure, I knew *how* to read but I didn't know *what* to read. I started going through the newspaper from front to back so I could comment with some intelligence about what was going on in the world. I spent my time off at the library and got my high school diploma. All that wouldn't have happened without Sean."

"I didn't know . . ." Kara's voice was soft.

"That's not all. More importantly, he trusted me and let me take over some of his responsibilities. Eventually, he let me buy into the business. I was pleased not just for the chance to own something at last but for the chance to be trusted. He offered me a partnership. No one had ever given me an opportunity like that before.

"He was more than a father to me, Kara. He was my whole family. He saved me. Without your dad, I'd be in jail or maybe even dead. He wanted me as a partner, Kara . . . but I'm not sure that he would have wanted me for you."

"Nick —"

"No, Kara, it's true. He called you his little girl, and he always hoped for the best for you. He loved me, Kara. But he knew who I was, where I came from, and I don't think he would have wanted that for you. He would have wanted someone who was good enough."

"Good enough for me?" Kara forgot that she was naked, got out of bed and crossed the space between them. "Nick, you're talking like someone out of another century."

She lowered herself into his lap, and Nick's arms instinctively went around her. "No, I'm not, Kara. I —"

She put her finger on his lips. "Listen to me. Sean was my father, so let me be the judge of what he would have wanted for me. Okay?"

"I knew him better than you did, Kara."

"Then I'm sure you knew that he wanted me to be happy."

"Of course." Nick shifted Kara on his lap. "That's what I just said."

"I am happy, Nick. And that's all that matters. I'm happy being with you." She snuggled in his arms and indulged herself in the warmth of his body. "Besides, Sean didn't know about magic."

"Magic?" Nick kissed her neck. He was beginning to forget about his argument.

"Yes, the magic that happens between two people who belong together." She kissed Nick on the mouth. "He didn't know how much I'd love kissing you." She nibbled at his lips. "Or hugging you." She wrapped her arms around his bare back, pressed her face against his cheek and delighted in the prickly sensation of his beard. "You didn't shave."

"No."

"I'm glad." She kissed his rough cheek. "Sean didn't know any of that. He didn't know how wonderful I feel when I'm with you in the night, Nick." She heard his breath catch. "Or how wonderful it is for you. It is wonderful, isn't it?"

Nick nodded.

"Then tell me, Nick," she whispered as she held onto him tightly. "Say it."

He took her face in his hands and looked deep into her eyes. "I love you, Kara. I love you more than anything in the world."

Kara smiled and slid off his lap. "In that case . . ."

"You want me to prove it?" Nick asked with a grin.

"That's what I had in mind." Kara reached out and took his hand to pull him with her to the bed. "The Sundowner's closed. . . ."

He kissed her mightily. "So we have all day."

The day turned to night, and the next time they woke up it was to another sunrise. They drifted out of sleep in each others' arms.

Nick was the first to get up. "Have to open the bar," he said, planting a kiss on her cheek. "The regulars get here early."

"Hmm." Kara turned over to watch him pull on his shorts. "I'll get up soon."

"Sure you will." Nick paused at the door to

look at her and Kara knew the message in his eyes would stay with her for a long time. It was one of love.

"Nick, I will," she insisted. "I'd miss you too much up here alone. Besides, today's the sweet sixteen party."

"Ah-ha, the real reason."

"Part of it, anyway." Kara sat up in bed. "It's not going to be easy without Arthur and Betty."

"Well, I have a surprise for you. They're back."

"What?"

"I heard them drive up early this morning, during that brief lull when you stopped seducing me long enough to doze off."

"Nick, you —" Kara heaved her pillow at him but missed by a mile.

Nick started laughing and couldn't seem to stop.

"Nick, what's so funny?"

"You could have gone ahead and thrown that vase the other night — and done no damage at all. What awful aim you've got."

Another pillow flew through the air but didn't come any closer. Kara could still hear him laughing as he headed down the hall. She got up and began dressing. They'd showered together in the middle of the night, and she still felt refreshed, although a little stiff and sore.

She walked down the stairs, smiling to herself, thinking about the wonderful long day and night they'd spent together, looking forward to the night ahead, for she couldn't imagine it without him.

Betty greeted her as Kara walked into the dining room, and there seemed to be an extra twinkle in the older woman's eye. Kara had a feeling she and Nick were no secret, but she wasn't about to get into it. Besides, Betty wasn't even supposed to be at the Sundowner.

"What in the world are you doing here?" Kara asked.

"Now that's a nice greeting." Betty put her hands on her hips and scolded Kara with pursed lips.

"Well, aren't you and Arthur supposed to be on your honeymoon?"

"My husband and I are going to be on our honeymoon for the rest of our lives," Betty said with slow relish. "So we just decided to get on back home where we belong. Also, I was worried about you and Michael trying to handle all these teenaged girls by yourself."

Impulsively, Kara gave Betty a big hug. "You're the best, and you're so right. We do need help. Where's Arthur?"

"Fussing in the kitchen."

"Oh, no."

"Well, now, Kara, what can you expect? The cleanup crew put everything back in the wrong place, or so he says. That's why he wanted to get back. Arthur just can't stand not being in control." Betty chuckled. "And he doesn't like it when Nick hires a relief chef. Says the standards go down overnight."

Betty walked beside Kara into the dining room where they began arranging flowers for the party. "Left over from your wedding," Kara said.

"And some wedding it was. You and Nick threw a real wonderful reception."

"We wanted to. After all, you're like family."

"The Sundowner is like a home to me. I think that had a lot to do with my coming back to Cypress Key. Of course, Arthur also played a role," she said with another chuckle. "But it's important to be with family, to feel like you belong."

Kara understood just what Betty meant. Home and family were so important. Betty belonged here with Arthur. And suddenly Kara realized that she belonged here, too. With Nick. At that moment she knew she had to get in touch with Larry Hartwell and stop him from putting any plans into motion. The Sundowner wasn't for sale.

After the sweet-sixteen partygoers departed in a swirl of pink streamers and gift wrap, Kara headed for the door, dropping her apron on the table by the cash register.

She arrived at Larry's office unannounced in the middle of the afternoon, probably his busiest time, but she was prepared to wait.

It didn't take long. Larry saw Kara and waved her in. "I'll be with you in just a minute," he told the man waiting in the lobby. Then to his secretary, "Hold my calls for a few minutes, will you, darlin'?"

Embarrassed at the looks she got from both client and secretary, Kara followed Larry into his office.

"Larry, I didn't mean for you to —"

"Don't worry about it. I've been meaning to call you and let you know what's happening — and take you to that dinner we missed."

"Larry, I've changed my mind."

"About dinner?"

"No, Larry, about the Sundowner."

There was a long pause. Kara sat down in the leather chair in front of the mahogany desk. Larry remained standing.

"You don't want to sell?" he asked.

"No, I don't. Everything's going really well. The new dining room is booming with business, and all the regulars have returned to the bar." She leaned forward in her chair. "I'm beginning to see why my father loved the Sundowner so much. The people there are like family to me now. We just had a wedding, and . . ."

"Wait a minute. Hold everything." Larry leaned back against his desk. "I'm a little confused about all this wedding and family talk. The last I heard, you wanted to dump the place."

"I did. Or I thought I did. But I've had a change of heart."

"Heart?" Larry spoke as if he'd never heard the word. "You can't let your heart rule your head where money is concerned, Kara."

"My head tells me the same thing," she said firmly. "We're making money, and we can make more. I want to make the Sundowner the most successful restaurant on the west coast. And I want to have fun doing it."

Larry walked around his desk and sat down in the swivel chair behind it. Several moments passed before he replied. "Well, now. I do wish you'd come by sooner, Kara. I've put some things in motion that I don't think we can stop."

"What things?" she asked nervously. Her palms were damp with perspiration.

"Like I told you, I made a few calls."

"Well, a few calls. If that's all —"

"And turned up a few interesting details," he added. "Details that we can't overlook, Kara."

Kara felt a horrible sinking sensation in her stomach.

"Are you with me, Kara?"

"Yes," she managed. "Go on."

"It seems the last time the Sundowner was inspected by the county, there were a couple of code violations that needed to be taken care of. Some new equipment had been added in the kitchen, and the electrical capacity hadn't been boosted to handle it. The whole electric panel needs to be torn out and rewired."

"Well, that's not so serious," Kara said hopefully.

"Not in itself. But that's only the beginning. There's a major problem with the plumbing. And the fire department's filed violations concerning the lack of adequate exits. All in all, it's not a pretty picture, Kara."

Larry reached for a file. He opened it and shuffled through the papers. "Just want to refresh my memory. Oh, yes. The county sent out an engineer to check the pilings. Part of the underpinnings on the southeast corner need to be shored up, which will mean lifting that whole section of the building. That in itself could cause structural damage to the subfloor."

Kara's throat was tight and dry. Her words were barely audible. "When . . . when did all this happen?"

"Just before your father's death, I believe. Because Sean was so popular, it looks like the various agencies gave him an extension. But the time is running out, Kara. They'll be checking the place out soon, and if the violations aren't taken care of, it'll more than likely be closed down."

"Closed down?"

"Looks like it. The place is worth nothing to developers, but they'd buy it in a minute, tear it down and put up condos, a hotel, whatever. We discussed that before, remember?"

Kara nodded. She felt as if she'd been punched in the stomach.

Unaware of her reaction, Larry continued his explanation. "So, when it gets condemned,

190

we'll step in and talk to Fleming about selling."

"Please, Larry —" Kara cleared her throat "— I want you to stop them," she said more firmly.

"Once those bureaucrats swing into action, there's not much chance of stopping them, Kara."

"You have to try," she demanded.

"Well, I'll call around, but I'm afraid that's about all I can do. Like I said, there's not much chance —"

"Do what you can, Larry. You started it, and I want you to stop it." Kara stood up, and Larry did the same.

"Let me remind you that I started it at your insistence."

"I realize that," Kara said, trying to keep her desperation from surfacing. "I made a mistake. Nick and I own the Sundowner together, and we want to keep it."

Without another word, Kara was out the door. She knew her feelings shouldn't be directed at Larry; he'd only done what she'd asked. But she hadn't expected him to move so swiftly, or with such vehemence. He almost seemed to delight in the problems he'd found at the Sundowner.

Kara headed for her car, aware that it was all her fault but not feeling any more kindly toward Larry because of it. She thought about getting in and just driving, not stopping, not looking back. But running wasn't the answer.

She had to go to Nick and tell him what she'd done. Together they could find a way to salvage the Sundowner. Maybe the violations weren't really that bad. Maybe they could correct them one at a time. Maybe it wouldn't be too expensive. Maybe. Maybe.

But Kara knew better. The violations Larry enumerated were serious.

Slumped behind the steering wheel, Kara shuddered. Nick would have to know what had happened, and telling him was going to be the hardest thing she'd ever done.

Kara sat out on the deck of the houseboat. Smoke from citronella candles kept the mosquitoes at bay. A faint breeze stirred the leaves of the live oak tree that hung over the water. A sliver of moonlight glinted across the deep, dark shadows of the river. The scene was tranquil and peaceful, and it reminded Kara of how much she'd come to enjoy her home on the river.

She was happy here now. That would have seemed impossible a few weeks before. But she'd quickly learned how to make the boat comfortable and it had been impossible not to enjoy the setting. She liked the peace and quiet of the river. There was a pair of egrets nesting downstream, and a family of raccoons played on the shoreline at night. She felt in harmony with the surroundings.

But tonight the tranquility was spoiled by the

turmoil that churned inside her as she waited for Nick. When she saw the Jeep's headlights, she felt a sense of relief. He was here. She'd face him and tell him everything. Together they'd find a way to save the Sundowner. It might not even be as bad as she thought, as bad as Larry had implied.

When Kara heard Nick whistling down the path, she suddenly didn't feel so secure.

"Kara —"

"I'm out here," she called.

The houseboat rocked in the water as he stepped on board and walked through to the deck.

"Hello there, nature girl." He dropped a kiss on her lips and held her close. When Kara fervently clung to him, Nick sneaked his hands inside the opening of her robe. "Great," he said. "Already undressed and waiting."

"Nick . . ."

"Yes?" He kissed her with leisurely thoroughness, his tongue making brief forays into her mouth.

"I need to . . . We need to . . ." She murmured the words against his mouth.

"I know," he said. "I really need to . . . And you need to . . ." He misunderstood her, and Kara knew it, but all the thoughts that had been swirling in her head stopped when he kissed her and held her close. She couldn't even remember them now. Kara could think of nothing but Nick, no one but Nick.

He guided her into the houseboat. The cool air inside was a delicious contrast to the heavy humid night. She felt the edge of the bed frame against her legs. Knees weak, but keeping her balance somehow, she sank down on the mattress. Nick untied her sash and her robe slid away from her body. His hands lingered at her breasts, his palms rubbing against her nipples as they peaked and swelled.

For a brief instant, a warning flashed through Kara's mind, but she couldn't hold on to the thought. She heard Nick's clothes rustle to the floor, then felt his body hard and strong beside her. His mouth was on her breast. At that moment Kara gave up any lingering pretense of rational thought. She and Nick were making love, and nothing else mattered. She never wanted it to end. . . .

He slid inside her, and she shifted her body to draw him in more deeply. She couldn't get enough of him; she'd never get enough.

Slowly, rhythmically, he moved inside of her, and Kara met his thrusts, arching toward him, fiercely wrapping her arms and legs around him. The tiny houseboat began to sway with their rhythms, the waves lapping against the side of the boat.

"I love you, Kara," Nick whispered. "I love you so much."

Kara wanted to answer, to tell him how she needed him and wanted him — and loved him. too. But they were so close to the moment of climax that words didn't matter now. They held the moment suspended between them, drawing it out as long as they could.

Deep inside, ripples of excitement grew and swelled until Kara was washed with an ecstatic torrent. It swept over her, and all she could do was give herself to it and let it engulf her totally just as it consumed Nick. They were on a wave of fulfillment that made them one in body and spirit. It was a perfect moment, and it went on and on, longer than either of them ever expected.

Nick held her close, their damp bodies pressed together. "How can it be possible?" he asked.

Kara looked up at him. "What, Nick?"

"Our lovemaking. Every time is better than before. In fifty years —"

Kara felt herself stiffen. She couldn't let Nick go on talking about the future when it was so uncertain.

Nick propped himself up on one elbow. "Hey, what is it? Don't you want to spend the next fifty years with me?"

Kara searched for a way to answer without alerting him to her concern.

"Or are you the kind of woman who's into one-night stands?"

He was teasing, but Kara heard the anxiety there, too. She fumbled for her robe and slid out of bed. It was dark, and she turned on a lamp that lit the room with a shadowy glow.

She saw his frown in the light.

"You're worrying me, Kara. You're making me wonder if you've decided to call everything off, go back to Atlanta —"

Tears began streaming down her face.

Nick swung his feet onto the floor and reached for her. "What is it? Why are you crying?"

Kara sank onto the bed and wiped futilely at her tears. "It's the Sundowner," she cried. "I've done an awful thing, Nick. I may have lost it for us."

Nick shook his head in confusion. "Lost it? What are you talking about? That's not possible."

"I hope not, but Larry Hartwell —"

"Hartwell, that slime. Anything to make a buck." He looked sharply at Kara. "What does he have to do with this?"

"I went to see him —"

"What?"

"It was weeks ago. I wanted to sell the Sundowner. You know that."

"Yes," Nick answered warily.

"But I didn't do anything about it until —"

Nick waited, silent.

"Until we had that fight and afterward made love. I was very confused then, and afraid. Mostly afraid. Larry said he would look into it and see what he could do to convince you to sell."

"Oh," Nick said carefully.

"Then everything changed and I guess I just didn't think about it again until Betty and Arthur came back. We were talking about family and —"

"Get to the point, Kara," Nick said abruptly.

"I went back to see him, to tell him I'd changed my mind."

"That was after you decided you loved me, right?"

"I loved you all along!" Kara defended. "I just didn't realize it."

"Go on. Tell me about Hartwell." Nick rested his head in his hands, not looking at her.

"Apparently he checked into the property and came across a report from the county. There were violations against the Sundowner."

"Violations?"

"Electric and plumbing and something about the pilings —"

"Oh, no." Nick stood up and grabbed his shorts. "I remember now. Sean told me about the report and said not to worry. He said they'd never move on it. After he died, I didn't hear anything more. Damn." He slammed his fist against the bulkhead.

"I'm sure that together we can work it all out." But her voice betrayed her doubt.

"Oh, are you?" Nick's voice was low and bitter.

"There was a six-month delay, Larry said. The time is almost up, but I just know that —"

"I don't want to hear any more of your

foolish predictions, Kara." His face was dark with anger. "What you don't understand is that a provisional six-month approval from Cypress County can last a lifetime. Unless some know-it-all big-shot real estate developer starts stirring things up."

"I hadn't thought of that."

"I'm sure you hadn't." Nick crossed the length of the houseboat in three strides and turned around to look at her.

Kara wrapped the robe tightly around her. She was beginning to shiver. "Sooner or later, wouldn't they have come back for another inspection?"

"What does that matter? It's sooner, now, thanks to you and your greed. Hell, this is what you wanted all along, isn't it, to ruin the Sundowner and get rid of me?"

"No!" Kara cried. "I mean it was, but it isn't now. I'm as upset as you. I just didn't realize how you were going to react."

"What did you expect me to do, Kara?"

"I don't know. I guess I thought we'd talk about it calmly, sit down together and think of what to do next."

"Next?" Nick spat out the word. "After you made a mess of everything."

"All right," Kara shot back. "Maybe I did, but I'm as upset about it as you are, Nick."

"Not too upset to go to bed with me," he observed dryly.

"That's not fair, Nick. You wanted it as much

as I did. Don't accuse me of seducing you."

"Sorry," he said tiredly. "That was low, but I'm so damned angry, Kara."

"I could be angry, too. I could even be accusatory. After all, you never bothered to check on any of the licenses or violations. You do have a way of letting things slide."

"You're absolutely right. This is all my fault, and I'm angry at myself. Does that make you feel better?"

"Nothing is going to make me feel better until we think of a way to save the Sundowner."

The look on Nick's face was of disbelief. "It's too late for that, Kara."

"I asked Larry to call off the county. He said he'd do what he could."

"I'm sure," Nick said sarcastically. "Don't you understand how he operates? He's looking for a big commission, and he won't get it if you don't sell. I wouldn't be surprised if he didn't grease a few palms to make sure our problems are beyond repair. We're going under, Kara."

She rose to approach him, but the dark, intense look in his eyes stopped her. She sat back down, momentarily deterred but still not defeated. "There has to be something I can do."

"Don't you think you've done enough?"

Kara's face fell. She knew she'd made an awful mistake, but she had hoped they could rectify it together. She hadn't expected him to turn on her.

Nick pulled on his sandals and reached for

his car keys. "There is something to be done. I'm calling Tommy Melendez."

"It's midnight, Nick."

"He gets paid for it."

Kara began putting on her clothes. "I'm coming with you. We —"

"Forget the 'we' stuff, Kara."

"But the Sundowner belongs to me, too."

"You should have thought about that when you paid your little visit to Larry Hartwell."

"I made a mistake, Nick. So did you. That's over. We have to go on from here."

"That's just what I'm doing. Without you."

With those words, Nick disappeared out the door and into the darkness.

11

"This is like a funeral," Michael grimly pronounced. Kara didn't like to hear it but knew he was absolutely right.

They were all gathered at the Sundowner. Kara, Michael, Melissa and Betty were slumped in chairs in the dining room; Buck, Arthur and Nick were near the bar, talking in low voices, their faces grim.

Throughout the Sundowner, upstairs and down, on the deck and under the building, inspectors representing various utilities, boards and agencies were poking around as if examining a terminal patient.

"I guess we have Larry Hartwell to thank for scheduling this invasion," Michael went on. "Wonder how he arranged to have all the inspectors arrive on the same day?"

"Because he has clout and power in the county," Melissa said glumly. "It's obvious that he wants to intimidate us and make us think everything's hopeless. Which is probably true." Her eyes were red from crying. "If we close, I guess I'll have to drop out of school for a while." She sank farther into her chair.

"Maybe not," Kara said abstractedly. She was cranky with worry and exhausted from trying to remain optimistic.

"There's not much out there." Melissa was the most despondent — and the most vocal — of the group. "I looked all over town before I started working here. Nothing but fast-food jobs for minimum wage and no tips. Can't pay rent and tuition on that. If I lose this job —"

"It's not lost yet," Betty piped in.

Kara looked at her gratefully. Betty had been her life raft in a sea of despair. Over the past few days, Kara had leaned heavily on her good-natured strength.

Michael was no less convinced than Melissa, just more stoic. "It probably is over if I know those guys from the county." He pulled his chair next to Melissa's. "You see, they let the Sundowner slide because of Sean. Now they're caught in dereliction of duty with Hartwell on their tails, so they have to make up for the past by being tough. They'll close us down within the week."

Kara felt sick. She hadn't been able to eat or sleep, and the sight of Nick's face, so hard and cold, tore at her heart. "I'm sorry," she said for the thousandth time.

"What's done is done." Betty was more philosophical than the young people.

"*We* should be doing something," Melissa cried.

"What?" Michael asked.

"I don't know." Melissa was about to cry again. "You can survive off of your wife's salary. But what about Buck?" She glanced toward the bar where the others were congregated. "He doesn't have a home or family. The Sundowner's his life."

"He'll find something," Betty said. "We all will. If it comes to that."

"What about you and Arthur?" Michael asked.

"We'll move on."

"At least you have skills. This job is the best I can do until I'm out of school," Melissa said.

"It may be the best I can do, period." Michael was picking up on Melissa's mood.

Kara couldn't stand any more. "I'm going outside for some air," she murmured.

She could hear Betty's admonition as she left. "Now you kids leave that girl alone. Can't you see her heart is breaking?"

Kara held onto the porch railing. The rough old wood gave her a feeling of stability, something to grab on to when everything around her was slipping away. And it was all her fault; no doubt about that. She'd been the catalyst who'd brought this disaster down on all of them, and in spite of Betty's words of defense, Michael and Melissa had a right to be upset. The Sundowner was their foundation. It was up to Kara to keep the place for them — for all of them. But how?

Nick came out on the porch but remained distant, at the far end. A subdued Topaz padded quietly after him and sat at his feet, looking up, eyes curious.

"What's happening?" Kara asked.

Nick stared over the water as he answered. "Worse than you'd predicted. Bad wiring, not enough exits, rot in the pilings. All that, plus the iron pipes have to be converted to copper and we need a sprinkler system."

"What?" Kara was confused.

"Not to water the plants, Kara." Nick spoke in a sharp voice. "It's an old frame building and in case of fire . . . Oh, never mind."

"What do you mean, 'never mind'? This is my place, too, Nick."

"Which is why we're here today, watching the ax fall."

All day Kara had been the target of accusations. Now it was about time she responded with some solutions. "I've been thinking about how we can raise the money for repairs. If we sell the houseboat and my car —"

"Both used and not in good condition," he countered. "A couple of thousand maybe. We need a lot of money, Kara. *A lot.*"

Tired of talking across the porch, Kara moved over to where Nick was standing. Topaz shifted so that he was sitting at her feet. "We can go to the bank. This is a profitable business so we should be able to get a loan on it for remodeling."

Nick's smile was tight. "Not when Larry Hartwell's father owns the damn bank."

"I didn't know that. But there're other towns and other banks," she argued. "We can try up and down the coast."

"I've thought of that. They'd say there's not enough collateral here, and you know it, Kara."

Kara hated to see Nick so bitter, but she knew he had reason. There was still one alternative. "I'll go to Atlanta to talk with my stepfather."

"I thought he didn't lend money."

"This time he has to." Kara felt determined and tried to convert that feeling into hope.

It didn't work for Nick. "Sure," he said flatly as he turned to go back into the restaurant.

"Nick —"

"Fine, Kara. Give it a try."

Kara watched him go. Feeling more alone than she ever had in her life, she sank slowly to the deck, arms wrapped around her knees. In a moment she felt a warm wet tongue licking at her cheek. Topaz snuggled up to her and, as Kara embraced him, her tears fell softly into the old dog's shaggy fur.

Buck was behind the bar when Nick returned inside. He was trying to look cheerful, but Nick could see the effort behind the smile. "Pour me a double, Buck."

"Little early in the day, isn't it?"

"Not under these circumstances. You're a good listener, right, Buck?"

"Well, I try to be, but you said recently that I talked too much."

"Now *I'm* going to."

"Go ahead, Boss."

"We don't have much chance here to meet the code, you know that, don't you?"

"Guess I do."

"We don't have the money." Nick took a gulp of his drink. "And we lack collateral to get the money."

Buck nodded.

"So Kara's going back to Atlanta to see if she can get a loan from her stepfather."

"Great." Buck leaned on the bar.

"There just one problem, Buck. I'm afraid if she goes, she might not come back." He waited, but Buck didn't respond. "I can see you also think that's a possibility. It's getting a little rough around here, too rough for Kara, maybe. The party's over, time to move on."

"Could be, Boss."

"Yep. It could be." Nick took another drink. "I've only gotten really close to two people in my life — Sean was one, and his daughter was the other. Sean left me."

"He died, Nick. He didn't want to leave you."

Nick went on. "After he was gone, Kara came along. Someone I thought I could make a life with. Now she's leaving. It seems to be a pattern with me, eh, Buck?"

Buck filled Nick's glass again in silence.

Kara had been in Atlanta two days, sleeping in the guest room at the Selwyns' townhouse on what had turned out to be a fruitless mission.

"Darling, I wish you wouldn't leave so soon."

Kara briefly looked up from her packing. "I found out what I needed to know, Mother. James won't give me a loan." Her stepfather had been as adamant as ever about his no-loan policy even though Kara had made a straightforward business appeal, promising him a healthy interest. He hadn't been moved.

"It's not that he doesn't love you, Kara." Janet Selwyn sank onto the bed. As always she was elegantly groomed, her hair perfectly coiffed, her silk blouse and linen skirt unwrinkled.

"I know that." Kara carelessly folded a skirt and stuffed it into her suitcase.

"I just don't understand," Janet said, "this obsession you have with a tatty old bar in Florida. It's not worth saving." She sniffed disdainfully, "I thought you wanted to run an art gallery. I thought that was the point of your going to Florida, to sell the place. Now that you *can* sell it, you don't want to." She threw up her hands in dismay.

"It seems weird to me, too, Mother. But the Sundowner is what I want, and I have a gallery there, sort of. At least, I've started showing the work of a few local artists and some of it is awfully good. It'll all come together in time, but first we have to save the building."

"Hmm." Janet smiled slyly. "I saw Deena

Caldwell at the club last week. She's opening a little antique shop in Decatur. It's going to be darling."

"I'm sure," Kara said abstractedly.

"She's looking for someone to run it. She asked about you, if you might be back in Atlanta soon."

Kara closed the lid on her suitcase. "I'm not available to run Deena's adorable boutique. I have a job running a restaurant, I hope. Anyway, I've sublet my apartment here, and I've settled in Cypress Key."

"In a houseboat." Janet arched her eyebrows.

"Which may have to be sold," Kara admitted. "That reminds me, I went by the bank to get the title to my car, and I took the pearls grandmother gave me out of my safe deposit box."

"Well, I'm glad you're finally going to wear them."

"I'm planning to sell them, Mother." She saw the pained look on Janet's face and bent to kiss her cheek. "I need the money. Nick and I need the money."

"We don't even know anything about this Nick person, where he's from, who his parents are . . ."

"I'm sure you'll like him." Kara glanced around the room. "What did I forget?"

"Now don't try to change the subject, darling. You're obviously serious about this man, too serious."

"Yes, I am serious. But don't dismiss him so

readily when you don't even know him, Mother."

"I know he runs a bar, just like your father. That's no life for someone like you, living hand-to-mouth."

Kara's plane was leaving in two hours; this wasn't the time for a heart-to-heart talk with her mother. But they'd avoided it for years, and the moment might never come again. Kara sat on the bed and put her arm around the older woman's straight, rigid shoulders.

"You and I are very different. We want different things out of life. You always wanted security —"

"A roof over my head, at the very least," Janet said bitterly. "And with Sean Gallagher, who ever knew?"

"I've learned a lot about Sean through the people whose lives he touched. He was a good man, Mother. Maybe not the man for you, but a loyal and kind man. I'm only sorry I didn't have more time with him."

Janet got up and went to the window, her back to Kara. "I've felt guilty about that, about keeping him from you, but James felt — and I did, too — that it would be confusing to divide your time that way. James wanted to be your father so much. He was proud when you took his name." She turned back to Kara. "I hope you're not bitter about this loan. You know that he'd *give* you the money if he thought it was in your best interest, a good investment for you."

"I know about James and his investments, Mother. They have to be rock-solid."

"He's careful, but he's always been very generous with you, Kara. You're the only daughter he ever had."

"But I'm Sean's daughter, too," Kara said softly. "Sometimes I wonder what it might have been like to have known him."

Janet's eyes were bright with tears. "I understand that. Sometimes I wonder, too, what it might have been like if I'd stayed with Sean."

Kara went to her mother, and they hugged each other tightly. Then, unexpectedly, Janet whispered, "Sean was an exciting man, you know. I've never forgotten that. You go to your exciting man, darling. I hope it works out for you."

"That flight has been cancelled," the agent said as Kara lugged her bags to the check-in counter.

"Canceled, why?"

"Weather conditions."

"But the weather's beautiful."

"There's a hurricane approaching your destination area."

Kara's mind flashed back to earlier that morning. She'd heard something on television about an approaching hurricane but had paid little attention when it didn't seem to be a threat. "It was heading out to sea."

"It's veered east, and we've canceled all

flights to the Gulf coast of Florida. Can I re-route you?"

"Where to?"

"Where would you like to go?"

"I'd like to *go* to Cypress Key." Kara was getting exasperated.

"Ma'am, I just told you —"

"I know," Kara said wearily. "Just get me as close as possible."

The agent checked her computer. "There's a flight to Miami in half an hour, but it's fully booked. If you'd like to stand by —"

"Fine." Kara handed over her ticket and waited impatiently as the agent reissued it for the Miami flight.

"If you don't make this one, you can continue standing by for the next flights — if they don't get canceled. The weather reports aren't good, even for the Miami area."

"I'll take a chance," Kara said as she grabbed the ticket and headed toward the gate.

She was the last stand-by to be called, and it wasn't until the plane took off that she had time to think about the threat to Cypress Key. It was too soon to worry. Hurricanes had a strange way of changing course or being downgraded to tropical storms.

Hurricane Ada, the first of the season, stayed right on course. By the time Kara's plane landed in Miami, the winds had picked up, and it was beginning to rain. All area flights were canceled. She had no choice but to check into a hotel.

For the next twelve hours, Kara was glued to the television set in her room, watching the destruction caused by the hurricane that plowed into Florida's west coast. The pictures were devastating. Waves pounded over seawalls, boats were overturned, houses demolished. Journalists swarmed to the coast to send out coverage of the storm, but there was no direct news from Cypress Key, reported to be the hardest hit.

Frantically, Kara called every number she knew in the town. They were all out of order. She was sick with worry not only about Nick but everyone at the Sundowner. It had all happened so fast; she could only hope they'd had enough warning to get away and head inland for safety.

Once Kara realized there was nothing to do but wait, she tried to calm down, ordered a sandwich from room service and then called her mother. Before hanging up, Kara assured her, "I love you, too, Mother. And Dad. Don't worry. I'll call when I get there."

Kara leaned back on the pillows and stared at the ceiling. She loved her parents and understood them. In a way, she'd gone back to Atlanta not just for the money but for the sense of safety and security she'd always known in that place. And she'd found out that she didn't want to live that way anymore.

Kara was relieved now that it was all over. James had turned her down, but what else did she expect? She knew he wasn't going to change character suddenly just because she wanted to save the Sundowner. She also knew her parents had kept her away from Sean not because they hated him but because they were afraid of losing Kara to him. James and Janet had lived their lives in emotional fear. They wouldn't change, but that didn't mean she couldn't.

Kara wasn't a little girl now, and she wasn't afraid. As much as she loved and respected her parents, she was on the way to forging her own life with her own set of values and goals. And Nick was at the center. She wanted to take chances, reach out and embrace life. And with Nick that would happen. This wild dash back to Cypress Key was only the first step.

By morning the worst was over, but the rain continued. Even in Miami there were signs of damage, shingles blown off roofs and broken branches cluttering the streets. Kara decided not to wait any longer. If there were no flights, she'd just rent a car and drive to Cypress Key.

It was midday before she got out of town, and halfway through her journey Kara wished she'd listened to the hotel clerk and the car rental agent, who'd advised she wait another day. The Everglades Parkway, which connected the east and west coasts of Florida, was a long, two-lane stretch of road nicknamed Alligator

Alley. With murky canals running along either side and frequent signs warning of bear or cougar crossings, it wasn't easy driving at the best of times. In a rainstorm, it was a nightmare.

With sweaty palms, a stiff neck and her heart in her throat, Kara finally made it to Naples, the Alley's western terminus. She pulled into a café for coffee, a sandwich and a brief rest. She'd managed to get this far, but she still had a long way to go. Even though traffic on the Interstate North was running smoothly, she was miles from her destination.

Kara left the café and drove on mechanically, the headlights of her car gleaming on the rainswept highway. Her mind played over a thousand disastrous scenarios of Nick and the Sundowner. When she neared the turnoff to Cypress Key the extent of the storm's damage finally hit her. The word "hurricane" had never meant much to Kara; it conjured up mental pictures of high tides on windswept beaches, overturned mobile homes and an occasional car crushed by a fallen tree.

It was all that and much more. She was stunned by the awesome power of the winds that had blown across the west Florida coast. Entire stands of pine trees had been destroyed, their trunks neatly snapped like toothpicks a few feet from the ground. Huge oaks that had been uprooted now lay still as corpses.

The closer she got to home the more frightened Kara became. Then she saw the police cars, their red lights flashing. It was a road-block, and it stretched across the highway that led to Cypress Key.

Kara rolled down the window.

"Sorry, ma'am, you'll have to turn back." Rain coursed down the bill of the young police-man's hat and along his shiny black slicker. He looked exhausted.

"Go back? I can't. I have to get through!"

"It's all closed down along the coast because of the wind and water damage. Electric wires are all over the road. It's too dangerous for sightseers."

"But I'm not a sightseer! I'm going home. I own the Sundowner."

He peered intently into the car. "The Sundowner, eh?"

"Yes, I'm Kara Selwyn, Nick Fleming's partner. Have you heard anything about the Sundowner?"

His lips tightened. "I don't have details on any of the structures along the coast, but it's real bad down there. I shouldn't let you through —"

"But please, Officer. I have to get home. My . . . my family's depending on me."

"Well, since you live there . . . But promise me you'll drive real careful. There's a crew clearing up along the coast road, and they may stop you again. Fact is, once you get close by the Sundowner, you may not be *able* to get through."

"Then I'll walk," Kara declared.

"Okay, ma'am, but just be careful, and avoid those wires, you hear?"

Kara gave the policeman a wave of thanks and drove slowly through the town. She watched amazed, as she passed whole blocks that had been untouched. Then, a few feet away, vacant, rubble-strewn lots appeared where buildings had once stood. The bank had been spared and the church across the street, although its steeple lay shattered on the ground. But the Palms Motel, where she'd spent her first nights in Cypress Key, was nothing more than a pile of broken glass and splintered wood. There didn't seem to be any rhyme or reason to the hurricane's path of destruction. She could only hope that the Sundowner had been spared the strongest of the capricious winds.

Even without the policeman's warning, Kara would have driven with extreme care, watching for live wires, pulling onto the shoulder to avoid fallen trees; she was too scared to do anything else. As she neared the Gulf, she saw the boats, not at anchor in the harbor but strewn along the shore as casually as a child might have tossed toys in a playroom. There was a twenty-foot sailboat on someone's front porch and a speedboat atop what was left of the bait shop. Nothing remained of the fishing wharf except a few spindly pilings. Telephone poles leaned drunkenly over the road.

There was a tight, cramped sensation in the pit of her stomach and her heart was pounding rapidly. As she drove through the devastation, Kara moved her lips in a whispered prayer. "Let Nick be all right. Please, God, let him have survived this horror."

She stopped the car and surveyed the road ahead. It was completely blocked, and a cleanup crew was at work. But Kara didn't need to drive any farther. She'd reached the Sundowner.

Or what was left of it.

She climbed out of the car. Immediately her shoes sank into the wet sand and rain slashed across her face. The Sundowner was a wild jumble of debris strewn across the sand.

Kara stifled a cry and stumbled into the rubble. Although it was late afternoon, the sky was dark, and she could barely see through the rain and mist. She searched around vainly for some sign of life. There was nothing.

Then a shadowy form appeared from behind a pile of splintered boards. She jumped, her pulse pounding wildly as it ran to her and almost knocked her off her feet.

She fell to her knees and clutched the wet, dirty dog. "Topaz! You're all right. Where's Nick? Find him for me."

For one maddening moment she had a premonition of Nick lying trapped beneath the rubble. On shaky legs she followed the dog, crawling over what had once been the shining teak bar, tripping through the twisted remains of Arthur's prize freezer, picking her way across a sea of broken chairs and tables.

"Nick, where are you?" Her words were blown away with the wind.

Something moved in the distance. She strained to see through the driving wind and rain and fought her way toward the crouched form, bent over, as if searching for something.

"Nick!"

He straightened, looked up at her and began to run, kicking rubble out of the way as he neared her.

"Kara, you're back. You're here!" His voice resonated with relief and joy.

She stumbled toward him with Topaz barking and jumping beside her. Then Nick's arms were around her, holding her close.

She clung to him, kissing him over and over. "You're all right," she cried. "Thank God you're all right. I was so scared."

"Yes, I'm all right." He cupped her head in his hands and stared down at her through the rain. "You're back, you're really back."

"Yes, Nick, darling. I would have been here sooner if I could have gotten through. Where did you go during the storm? What happened to everyone else — ?"

"They're all fine. We had a warning in time and headed inland for cover." Nick surveyed the soggy, pathetic remains of the Sundowner,

"I never imagined this would happen."

"What matters is that everyone's all right," Kara said firmly. "We can start all over, Nick."

Nick bent down and picked up a shard of pottery. "My coffee cup," he said, "or a piece of it. That's what I've been doing today, wandering around, trying to find something to hold on to."

"You have something," Kara said. "You have me to hold on to."

He embraced her tightly. "But I can't take you home with me, darling," he murmured. "This is what's left of home."

"We have the houseboat," Kara asserted. Then she panicked. "Don't we?"

Nick started to laugh loudly, his head thrown back. Astounded, Kara asked, "Nick, what is it? What's the matter? Stop it, you're scaring me."

"We have a houseboat, but there's just one problem," Nick answered, still laughing.

"What?"

"It's sitting in the middle of Kyle's garden. He's a little upset about it. His tomato plants will never be the same." Nick broke into laughter again.

Struck by the absurdity of their desperate situation Kara joined in. Together they sank to the wet ground, arms around each other, laughing into the wind and rain until tears ran down their cheeks.

"Don't say it, Kara," he warned as he wiped the tears and raindrops from her face. "Don't say we have everything we need — each other, the sun in the morning, the moon at night. I don't think I could take that right now."

"But it's true," she countered. "We do have each other, and that's all I care about. Our friends are fine, and we have a very wet and sandy, but healthy, dog. We can live in the houseboat until we rebuild the Sundowner —"

She saw the quick change of expression on Nick's face. "We are going to rebuild, aren't we?" she asked. Nick didn't respond. "In a way, this hurricane is the answer to our prayers, isn't it?" Still there was no answer. "We can rebuild up to the proper standards and tell Larry Hartwell to take a hike. I'm sure the insurance will — oh, no . . ." She drew in a deep shuddering breath. "You didn't forget to pay the insurance?"

"No, I didn't forget. I didn't have to. Sean had the insurance paid up and left the policy with Tommy. We checked it this afternoon. We're insured but not for nearly what it would cost to rebuild. Sean had a theory that insurance companies overcharged so he chose the lowest rate and the highest deductible. And I went right along with it."

"We will get some money? Please tell me that."

"Some." He hugged her tightly. "Now I'm beginning to feel like the one who'd be happy with the sun, the moon, and you. We could rebuild, Kara — something just about the size of a stand to sell Arthur's shrimp rolls from. But we could never rebuild it anything like the way it was."

Kara pushed Nick's damp hair away from his forehead. Despite all the bad news, she suddenly felt as though they'd won. "Maybe that's good. Maybe we should take the money and try something different."

"We?" Nick looked around in the rainy twilight gloom. "You can look at this . . . this mess and still say 'we'? I came here ten years ago with nothing, Kara. And here I am again, with nothing."

"I'm not leaving you, Nick Fleming, never again. I'm sticking to you like glue. So what do you think of that?"

He leaned forward and kissed her wet lips. "I think you're crazy."

"Well, at least I'm not so crazy I laugh hysterically because a houseboat is in the middle of a vegetable garden."

"You're just so crazy you want to live with a destitute man — in a boat in the middle of a vegetable garden."

"You bet I do." Kara grabbed Nick's hand.

He pulled her to her feet and put his arms around her. They clung together, oblivious of their rain-soaked clothes. Finally, with one arm still around Kara's shoulders, Nick led her out of the rubble.

Then he stopped and whistled loudly. "Come on, Topaz. We're going home. "

Epilogue

Two days had passed. The June sun shone dazzlingly on the turquoise blue waters of the Gulf. Kara shielded her eyes to watch a trio of gulls circling in the cloudless sky.

She'd spent the morning with Nick and Tommy Melendez discussing options for the Sundowner property. Tommy was optimistic that the destroyed buildings of Cypress Key would be rebuilt and the town would come back stronger than ever. He was also realistic enough to warn Kara and Nick that the insurance money wouldn't be adequate to replace the Sundowner. He suggested that they consider selling the land to a developer and relocating their bar on less expensive property somewhere else.

But it wouldn't be the same, Kara told herself as she returned to the task of sorting out a drawer of silverware and cutlery she'd stumbled upon. Most of the Sundowner's employees had joined them to sift through the rubble and salvage what they could before the county demolition team arrived to clear the lot.

The wrath of the hurricane had been strangely selective. Nick's clothes were gone, but his shoes, which he seldom wore, remained in pristine condition. Books and records were ruined, but an entire set of china had survived. So had a case of ripe olives, which Betty opened with a flourish and set out along with sandwiches she'd made for their final day on the site.

Now, by late afternoon, their group had dwindled to three — Nick, Kara and Arthur — the others having gone home for a shower and a change of clothes. Topaz, who'd started out with abundant energy, had grown weary of digging through the debris and now dozed in a shady nook under a toppled piling.

Kara looked up when she heard Arthur call, "Hey, Nick, Kara, come and see what I've found." He was holding a battered steel box, securely fastened with a lock.

"What is it?" he asked Nick.

"It's Sean's safe." Nick took the box from Arthur. "Years ago, he took me down to the storeroom and showed it to me."

"And you never opened it?" Kara asked.

"I forgot all about it. Funny," Nick said, examining the box. "He gave me a key that day and said there'd come a time when the safe should be opened."

"Where's the key?" Arthur asked.

Nick shrugged. "With the rest of my stuff, somewhere in this rubble." He shook his head and told Kara, "I guess that's typical of me, putting things off, forgetting about the business end of our partnership."

"Well, it wasn't a strong point of yours — or

Sean's," Arthur reminded him. "But he said there'd come a time, and I guess the time is now."

Kara was impatient. "Enough talk. Let's open it and see what's inside." She found a rock and handed it to Nick. "Can you break the lock?"

Nick put the box on the ground. "I'm sure I can," he said, hesitating.

"Go ahead, Nick. I can't stand the suspense," Kara urged.

"You do it, Arthur," said Nick.

The big man wasn't so hesitant. He took the rock and began pounding on the lock until it shattered. He pulled it off and stood up. "You have to open it," he told Nick.

"No, I —"

"Nick, go ahead!" Kara urged. "He told you there'd come a time."

"I know, but —"

"What's the matter?" Kara asked.

"Aren't you even curious?" Arthur added. Kara and Arthur prodded him, but Nick still held back. "I'm sure there's nothing important in it. Probably just some personal things."

"But he told you —"

"I know, Kara, but I don't feel right. Sean was your father."

"And your friend."

"He didn't know you'd be here when the time came to open it."

Arthur bent down and picked up the safe.

"Maybe he did." He offered it to Kara, who reached out, aware that her hands were shaking. She understood suddenly how Nick felt. It seemed so personal, this last relic of her father's. Finally she pried it open.

There was a manila envelope on top, wrapped with string. She untied it and took out the contents. "There're photos. Pictures of me as a baby." She sifted through them. "Me and my mother. Oh, Nick, look. Letters I wrote to him when I was little. I remember this one." She examined the childish scrawl.

"There're some more papers here," Nick said, reaching into the safe at last. He pulled out several sheets and another envelope. "This has your name on it." He handed it to Kara just as Arthur let out a muffled cry.

"Look!"

"What in the —" Nick was pale.

"I don't believe it," Kara whispered.

The bottom of the box was filled with money, neat stacks of hundred-dollar bills. Kara, Nick and Arthur stared at one another in stunned silence.

Kara sank down onto a pile of bricks, still holding the letter as Nick and Arthur took out the bills. "I've never seen so much money." Arthur began a rough count. "Nick, there must be thousands."

"Just like Sean to have a stash. He never trusted banks."

"Where'd it come from? You suppose Sean

robbed a bank without telling us?" Arthur chuckled.

Kara only half listened as she tore open the envelope. "It's a letter."

"Read it, Kara." Nick put his arm around her shoulder while Arthur stood aside, still holding the box full of money.

Kara carefully unfolded the letter.

Dear Kara,

I won't be around when you open this, but I want you to know I've always loved you and wanted you to have the best. That's why I gave in to your mom and stepfather. They could do a lot more for my little girl than an old guy in a run-down bar. That's what I thought then. Now I see that I was wrong. I wish I'd fought harder for you. I wish it had been different, but wisdom comes with age.

Kara stopped reading and looked up at Nick. "I said the same thing to Mother, that I wished Sean and I could have had more time together."

Nick slipped his arm down to her waist and pulled her closer. "Go on. Let's hear the rest."

"It's about you, Nick." Tears filled Kara's eyes as she read.

A few years ago a young man wandered into the Sundowner and made himself at home. I guess both of us were lonely and wanted a family. Nick needed something of his own, and I would have given him part interest in the Sundowner, but he wouldn't have accepted it that way. So he started paying me. I didn't have any use for the money — it never meant much to me — as your mom will tell you. I saved most of it, saved it for you, Kara. There was a time when I thought I'd give it to you on your wedding day and maybe you'd even let your old dad walk you down the aisle.

Kara's voice broke at that, and she clung to Nick. He took the letter and finished it in a voice that was less than steady. Arthur was crying openly, tears streaming down his cheeks.

So, little girl, here it is to use however you decide. Just remember your old dad loved you very much.

For a long time no one spoke. Arthur stood silently crying.

Kara finally spoke in a hoarse voice, almost to herself. "It's like a miracle, not just finding the money, but finding it now. If I'd opened that box when I first came to the Sundowner, who knows what would have happened?"

"What's going to happen now, Kara?" Arthur asked huskily.

"She doesn't have to decide anything yet." Nick had moved a few inches away to give her

227

some space. It was her money; it had nothing to do with him and Arthur.

Kara's eyes sparkled with something more than tears. "Oh, I've decided. Don't you want to know, Arthur?"

"Sure, I do!"

"But I don't think Nick does. Maybe I should keep him in suspense."

"Don't you dare." Arthur handed her the box.

Kara looked down at the money. "I'm going to — we're going to — rebuild the Sundowner."

"New and modern?" Arthur asked. "All shiny bright?"

"Nope." Kara was emphatic. "Just the way it was before, kind of like a grand old lady beyond her prime. I want it to be the same — for Sean and all the people who loved him and the Sundowner over the years. There'll have to be one change, though. The upstairs apartment will be larger, to accommodate one big old dog and the two people who're going to live there." Kara looked at Nick. "If you're willing to compromise and share it with me."

"Sean wouldn't approve of you living in the apartment with me —"

Kara felt her heart beating nervously. "Nick, we went through that before . . ."

"Unless we're married."

She threw her arms around his neck. "I think that can be arranged."

Arthur laughed in delight. "We sure know how to put on a wedding at the Sundowner. Can't wait to get home and tell Betty. And wouldn't Sean be happy to hear the news?"

Arthur's words were wasted on Kara and Nick, who were lost in the depths of a kiss.

The sun that had been poised on the brink of the Gulf began to slip below the horizon. Reds and golds and purples lit up the sky and wrapped Kara and Nick in a brilliant glow.

"Let's go, Topaz," Arthur said. "It's time for us to take a walk on the beach. I don't think Nick and Kara will mind us leaving them."

And they didn't.